MW01687134

Chan… his …cucumber.

He chuckled when he thought of the way she'd handled his daughter, Phil.

Little Phil had mustered a full frontal attack on Jolie. Usually the girl was more subtle about fending off prospective moms, but then, Jolie was different, and Phil knew it as well as Channing did.

More and more, Jolie Winters seemed to be just what he'd been looking for.

She wasn't into romance, but that could work to his favor. He'd tried the romance route, and that had been a disaster. He was more interested in a calm, sensible arrangement himself.

Why shouldn't marriage be as forthright and logical as business?

Yes, Jolie Winters was exactly what Channing was looking for….

Dear Reader,

Though August is already upon us, we've got yet another month of special 20th anniversary titles sure to prolong your summer reading pleasure.

STORKVILLE, USA, our newest in-line continuity, launches this month with Marie Ferrarella's *Those Matchmaking Babies.* In this four-book series, the discovery of twin babies abandoned on a day care center's doorstep leads to secrets being revealed...and unsuspecting townsfolk falling in love!

Judy Christenberry rounds up THE CIRCLE K SISTERS with *Cherish the Boss,* in which an old-school cowboy and a modern woman find themselves at odds—and irresistibly attracted to each other! In Cara Colter's memorable VIRGIN BRIDES offering, the "world's oldest living virgin" meets the man she hopes will be her *First Time, Forever.*

Valerie Parv's THE CARRAMER CROWN continues, as a woman long in love with Michel de Marigny poses as *The Prince's Bride-To-Be.* Arlene James delights with *In Want of a Wife,* the story of a self-made millionaire who is looking for a mother for his adopted daughter—and, could it be, a wife for himself? And Natalie Patrick offers the charming *His, Hers...Ours?,* in which a marriage-wary pair play parents and discover they like it—and each other—far too much.

Next month, look for another installment of STORKVILLE, USA, and the launch of THE CHANDLERS REQUEST...from *New York Times* bestselling author Kasey Michaels.

Happy Reading!

Mary-Theresa Hussey

Mary-Theresa Hussey
Senior Editor

Please address questions and book requests to:
Silhouette Reader Service
U.S.: 3010 Walden Ave., P.O. Box 1325, Buffalo, NY 14269
Canadian: P.O. Box 609, Fort Erie, Ont. L2A 5X3

In Want of a Wife

ARLENE JAMES

Silhouette
ROMANCE™
Published by Silhouette Books
America's Publisher of Contemporary Romance

If you purchased this book without a cover you should be aware that this book is stolen property. It was reported as "unsold and destroyed" to the publisher, and neither the author nor the publisher has received any payment for this "stripped book."

SILHOUETTE BOOKS

ISBN 0-373-19466-8

IN WANT OF A WIFE

Copyright © 2000 by Deborah Rather

All rights reserved. Except for use in any review, the reproduction or utilization of this work in whole or in part in any form by any electronic, mechanical or other means, now known or hereafter invented, including xerography, photocopying and recording, or in any information storage or retrieval system, is forbidden without the written permission of the editorial office, Silhouette Books, 300 East 42nd Street, New York, NY 10017 U.S.A.

All characters in this book have no existence outside the imagination of the author and have no relation whatsoever to anyone bearing the same name or names. They are not even distantly inspired by any individual known or unknown to the author, and all incidents are pure invention.

This edition published by arrangement with Harlequin Books S.A.

® and TM are trademarks of Harlequin Books S.A., used under license. Trademarks indicated with ® are registered in the United States Patent and Trademark Office, the Canadian Trade Marks Office and in other countries.

Visit Silhouette at www.eHarlequin.com

Printed in U.S.A.

Books by Arlene James

Silhouette Romance

City Girl #141
No Easy Conquest #235
Two of a Kind #253
A Meeting of Hearts #327
An Obvious Virtue #384
Now or Never #404
Reason Enough #421
The Right Moves #446
Strange Bedfellows #471
The Private Garden #495
The Boy Next Door #518
Under a Desert Sky #559
A Delicate Balance #578
The Discerning Heart #614
Dream of a Lifetime #661
Finally Home #687
A Perfect Gentleman #705
Family Man #728
A Man of His Word #770
Tough Guy #806
Gold Digger #830
Palace City Prince #866
**The Perfect Wedding* #962
**An Old-Fashioned Love* #968
**A Wife Worth Waiting For* #974
Mail-Order Brood #1024
**The Rogue Who Came To Stay* #1061
**Most Wanted Dad* #1144
Desperately Seeking Daddy #1186
**Falling for a Father of Four* #1295
A Bride To Honor #1330
Mr. Right Next Door #1352
Glass Slipper Bride #1379
†*A Royal Masquerade* #1432
In Want of a Wife #1466

*This Side of Heaven
†Royally Wed

Silhouette Special Edition

A Rumor of Love #664
Husband in the Making #776
With Baby in Mind #869
Child of Her Heart #964
The Knight, the Waitress and the Toddler #1131
Every Cowgirl's Dream #1195
Marrying an Older Man #1235
Baby Boy Blessed #1285

Silhouette Books

Fortune's Children
Single with Children

The Fortunes of Texas
Corporate Daddy

ARLENE JAMES

grew up in Oklahoma and has lived all over the South. In 1976 she married "the most romantic man in the world." The author enjoys traveling with her husband, but writing has always been her chief pastime.

IT'S OUR 20th ANNIVERSARY!

We'll be celebrating all year, Continuing with these fabulous titles, On sale in August 2000.

Intimate Moments

#1021 A Game of Chance
Linda Howard

#1022 Undercover Bride
Kylie Brant

#1023 Blade's Lady
Fiona Brand

SECRETS!
#1024 Gabriel's Honor
Barbara McCauley

#1025 The Lawman and the Lady
Pat Warren

#1026 Shotgun Bride
Leann Harris

Desire

#1309 The Return of Adams Cade
BJ James

#1310 Tallchief: The Homecoming
Cait London

#1311 Bride of Fortune
Leanne Banks

#1312 The Last Santini Virgin
Maureen Child

#1313 In Name Only
Peggy Moreland

#1314 One Snowbound Weekend...
Christy Lockhart

Special Edition

#1339 When Baby Was Born
Jodi O'Donnell

#1340 In Search of Dreams
Ginna Gray

#1341 When Love Walks In
Suzanne Carey

#1342 Because of the Twins...
Carole Halston

#1343 Texas Royalty
Jean Brashear

#1344 Lost-and-Found Groom
Patricia McLinn

Romance

#1462 Those Matchmaking Babies
Marie Ferrarella

#1463 Cherish the Boss
Judy Christenberry

#1464 First Time, Forever
Cara Colter

#1465 The Prince's Bride-To-Be
Valerie Parv

#1466 In Want of a Wife
Arlene James

#1467 His, Hers...Ours?
Natalie Patrick

Chapter One

Jolie crossed her long, bare legs and glanced at her watch. Two hours since she'd stood squarely in front of the fastidious desk of Channing Hawkins's fastidious secretary and belligerently declared that she would not leave until she had seen the great man himself, appointment or no appointment. Fat lot of good it had done her, too.

It wasn't, she reflected grumpily, that she hadn't tried to get an appointment. For weeks and weeks she'd begged to meet in person with anyone at Phillips Hawkins Computers who could tell her why her company of Austin 3 should not be allowed to make a pitch for the promotional contract for the much anticipated new PH personal computer. For weeks and weeks she'd been politely—and sometimes not so politely—rebuffed. In desperation she'd written letter after letter of protest and received what amounted to a pile of form rejections, saying, more or less, "Don't call us, kid. We'll call you."

Her fledgling agency was trapped in the proverbial vicious circle: If you haven't done a major campaign, you can't get a major campaign. Something had to give. And soon.

And it was up to her, as Contracts Manager and Head of Sales, to make it happen.

The secretary, whom Jolie had mentally nicknamed Fastidious Efficiency, smoothed the sleek roll of pale blond hair on the back of her sleek head with pale, pink-tipped fingers and aligned the message pad next to her telephone with the ink blotter in the center of her desk as if the accuracy of its placement would determine the fate of the free world. Having arranged her desktop to her satisfaction, the secretary then studiously turned her back on Jolie and began pecking at the keyboard of her PH Magnum computer. She had been efficiently ignoring Jolie since coolly refusing to allow her to speak with her boss, the principal stockholder and CEO of Phillips Hawkins. She had refused even to ask Channing Hawkins if he could work Jolie into his busy afternoon schedule. Although, as far as Jolie could tell, Hawkins had had no visitors and taken no phone calls since she'd parked her behind in this stiff, uncomfortable chair.

It felt as if someone had upholstered a collection of splintered boards and put them together with nails that were too long. Jolie shifted uncomfortably, and suddenly she had had enough. She looked to the door that stood between her and Channing Hawkins and knew that he was in there. When Fastidious Efficiency had moved in and out of his office, she had glimpsed him behind his desk, a tall, thin man with sandy brown hair and glasses. It was time, past time, that she made the acquaintance of Chan Hawkins. What, after all, did she have to lose? Sucking a deep breath through flaring nostrils, she picked her briefcase from the floor and got to her feet.

"You can't go in there!"

Chan heard his secretary's shrill voice raised to glass-shattering decibels just before the door to his office slammed open. He whirled around in his leather chair, away from the computer monitor, and peered over the tops of his glasses at the tall, willowy redhead framed in the open doorway, the strap of a soft valise slung over one shoulder. His first thought was, *Nice legs.* His second was, *Nice everything.* Then Phoebe shoved past her and huffily exclaimed that she was phoning security.

He cleared his throat. "What's the problem?"

Phoebe was in high dudgeon. Her normally pale cheeks were flying bright flags of color. Any disruption of her carefully scripted day usually left Phoebe seething, though she was much too prim and proper to give full vent to those carefully tamped emotions. She tugged on the hem of her pink, double-breasted suit coat and lifted her surgically sculpted chin. Channing often wondered how Phoebe had survived fifty-odd years of life with her perfectionist tendencies. Life, in his experience, was far from perfect, unless one counted those rare, special moments that seemed to come along unexpectedly—and he sincerely doubted that Phoebe did.

"She doesn't have an appointment," Phoebe said, enunciating each word crisply.

The redhead folded her arms, glaring daggers at Phoebe. Chan noticed that the woman's creamy, freckled skin flushed becomingly. For some reason, he felt like smiling, but instead cleared his throat again and schooled his expression. He made himself look away from the redhead in her cool, tailored, long-sleeve mint-green dress that revealed a slender shape and long, long legs. Removing his glasses, he leaned back on one elbow and addressed his secretary with genuine curiosity.

"Why didn't you give her an appointment?"

Phoebe flushed crimson. "Because," she spat, "she should have dealt with marketing."

"I *tried* to deal with marketing," the redhead snapped. "For *weeks* I've tried to deal with marketing."

Chan sighed inwardly. He liked to think of himself as a hands-on leader, but the truth was that he had his hands on research and development a lot more than on any other department. The truth was, he'd be lucky if he could keep a finger in all the departments, the company had grown that much. Heck, these days PH had departments of which he was all but unaware. Maybe he should listen to what this woman had to say. She had a deep, husky voice that wasn't at all hard to hear.

"I have a few minutes," he commented, trying hard not to look at anyone. "You can hold off security until I hear what she has to say, Phoebe."

As expected, Phoebe was incensed. Whirling away, she choked down a protest and swept through the door, dislodging their visitor as smoothly as a front-end loader. The instant the door closed at the redhead's back, Chan gave her his full attention. She was worth his full attention.

Her chin-length, flaming red hair had been swept back from her squarish face in ripples and waves and tucked behind her small ears. As a result, her slanted light brown eyes, carefully made up with earth-brown shadow and mascara, looked mysteriously exotic beneath flat, slender brows. Her mouth was small but plump and a luscious apricot color. The jut of her chin signified stubbornness, the apples of her cheeks hinted at a face-lighting smile, and the height of her forehead suggested intelligence. It was a face of incongruous parts, the only perfect feature being her straight, slender nose, yet it worked together into a pleasing whole. Added to a long graceful neck and a long, graceful body, it made for a very pleasing package, indeed.

Chan decided to play the part of gentleman. Getting to his feet, he leaned across the desk and offered her his hand. She jerked slightly, obviously surprised, then briskly stepped up and placed her hand in his. It felt cool and slender and oddly delicate.

"Channing Hawkins," he said needlessly, "and you are?"

"Jolie Winters of Austin 3."

He kept her hand in his for his next question, too, just because he wanted to. "And Austin 3 would be?"

"An advertising and publicity agency."

"Ah." He released her and nodded toward the single chair placed squarely in front of his desk. It matched the one in the waiting room and had been chosen, frankly, for its lack of comfort. Chan generally preferred to be left to his computer and schematics. As she lowered herself gingerly into the chair, he dropped into his comfortable leather executive model and resumed his habitual slump, templing his fingers, his elbows braced on the arms of his chair. "Go on," he said. "Tell me what's got you storming my office door."

She took a deep breath, nostrils delicately flaring, then made an irritated gesture. "Your marketing department wouldn't talk to me."

He didn't doubt it, but she'd found a way to make herself heard anyway, and he couldn't help admiring that. "I'm talking to you. Rather, I'm listening to you."

He watched her quickly assess him, up close and personal, and knew the instant she decided how to proceed. It was a spark in those iced-tea-colored eyes, a flash of intelligence that he had good cause to recognize. He'd been seeing the same thing in the face of his nine-year-old adopted daughter since the day he'd first held her in his arms. The recognition gave him a start, sent a spurt of excitement through him.

Jolie Winters shifted forward, crossing her long—and surprisingly bare—legs. "Listen, Mr. Hawkins, it's common knowledge that you're about to launch the most eagerly awaited PC in market history. Every major ad shop from New York to Seattle is cooking up a campaign. All I'm asking is that the hometown kids get an even shake. Let us show you what we can do, for pity's sake! Don't just slam the door in our faces before we even get a chance to make a case. Sure, we're small, but we're also hungry, and we've got major talent. Plus, we'll give you the best financial deal you've ever had. The big houses are going to want big bucks, but we need a chance to make a name for ourselves. Just let us show you what we can do, and if the bean brains in your marketing department still can't recognize a winner when they see one, well, then that's that, isn't it? But at least we'll have had a fair shot. What can it hurt? Come on."

She was passionate in her presentation, and she made a good case. He'd already decided to let her have a shot, but saying so now would be entirely too easy and not at all to his best interests.

"What about production money?"

"Ten thousand dollars," she said quickly. "The big houses probably got ten times that much."

Actually, they hadn't. Phillips Hawkins had never paid for bid production. Their first computer had dominated the market through sheer word of mouth, and they'd been solicited by every ad man with an idea since, but Channing remembered a time when ten thousand bucks had meant the difference between building computers as a hobby and building computers as a business. That same amount was chump change to him now, but before he parted with it, he'd be sure she understood what she was getting into.

He glanced needlessly at the calendar on his desk and said, "I can give you eight days. That means the presentation has to be in my hands by next Friday."

The whir of the cogs spinning in her brain was almost audible. She was calculating at the speed of sound. "Agreed."

He had to work at keeping his smile under cover. "By the end of business on Friday, then. And I'm not impressed by suits, Ms. Winters. Leave the other warm bodies at the shop and bring me the presentation yourself. Understood?"

She didn't bother to even think that one over. "Understood."

"I'll have accounting cut you a check. You can pick it up tomorrow."

For a moment she just sat there, staring at him, her mouth slightly ajar, but then she smiled, and the results were breathtaking: strong white teeth, apple cheeks, dimples. Best of all, those soft brown eyes lit like candles. She lurched to her feet.

"You won't regret this, Mr. Hawkins, I promise you!"

He was amused at the addition of the title. Her good-old-boy tack had yielded the desired results, but she'd quickly forgotten it in favor of respect the moment it had.

"We'll see."

"Dessie and Ben, my partners, are brilliant, the best creative team since, well, Rogers and Hammerstein!"

He did grin now; he couldn't help it. "I trust we won't be dealing with song and dance."

"What? Oh!" She laughed, and the smoky sound of it brushed across his nerve endings like silk and water. "No! I only meant... Well, you know what I meant."

He let his smile answer for him. An odd thing happened

then. She tilted her head as if really seeing him for the first time. The next instant, she stepped back, right into the chair. Quickly recovering her balance, she sidestepped, blinked, and was suddenly all business again. She stuck out her hand. "Thank you."

He shrugged and got up out of his chair. Clasping her hand, he held rather than shook it. "Friday, at the end of business."

"Absolutely."

She tugged her hand from his and backed toward the door.

"Uh, maybe you'd better leave me a card."

"A card," she repeated blankly. "Oh! A business card. Yes, of course."

She slung the satchel off her shoulder and flipped open the top. Quickly extracting the card, she held it out to him. He took it and glanced at it. Flat white with A3 and her name embossed in gold, the pertinent company information in black. He turned the card over in his hand. "Is it, uh, Miss or Mrs. Winters?"

She went on alert. "Why do you ask?"

He looked her straight in the eye. "Because I want to know."

She was silent a moment. "Miss." She lifted her chin in challenge. "I've never been married."

"Excellent." He tossed the card to the center of his desk blotter, bringing his hands to his waist. "See you in eight days, Miss Jolie Winters."

She nodded smartly, just once, and then she was out the door. He reached for the intercom switch, intending to distract Phoebe in order to spare Jolie Winters the sharp edge of her sharp tongue. He needn't have worried. Before the door swung closed again, he saw Jolie Winters stride by Phoebe's desk with a glare that could freeze mercury.

Phoebe literally shrank back, momentarily ignoring the buzzer. It was all Chan could do to keep the chortle out of his voice as he ordered his uptight secretary to have accounting cut a check for Austin 3. He was still smiling long after she'd reluctantly agreed to do so. It wouldn't do to get his hopes up just yet, of course, but instinct told him that he'd finally found the one. And instinct rarely failed him.

"Mommy?"

The hopeful sound of the small, drowsy voice tore at Jolie's heart and warned of difficulty to come. She got up from her desk and crossed the room to the small pallet where baby Mona had been napping the past hour or so, not nearly long enough for Jolie to actually get any work done, but a welcome respite from the exhausting business of watching over a toddler. Jolie couldn't understand how Dessie managed all alone.

"Mommy is still in the studio, darling," she said, going down on her knees next to the pallet. "But Jolie is here."

"No," Mona said sullenly and rolled onto her side, face crumpling in tears as a thin wail rose from the pallet. Jolie felt rather like crying with her. They were all exhausted. Dessie and their partner Benny had worked around the clock on the Phillips Hawkins concept, while Jolie had concentrated on the financial end of the contract, worried constantly about the impending deadline, and tried to keep Dessie's little daughter, Mona, happy, usually without notable success.

Dessie, whose real name was the unlikely moniker of Desdemona, had been bringing her little namesake to work with her ever since the day they'd opened the door on the old warehouse containing the small suite of bare-bones offices, studio, production stage, sound booth, editing room and computer room. Dessie was the creative genius, the idea maker, the concept dreamer. Benny, with his wide-ranging technical expertise, turned the concept into tangible reality. Jolie kept the show running day to day, balancing bank accounts, squeezing pennies, figuring bids and costs, drawing up contracts. She sometimes wished she had an accounting degree to go along with those of business administration and business law. At this moment, however, she'd have given her eye teeth for a degree in child psychology.

"I'm sorry, baby," she crooned, patting her chubby back.

Mona promptly rolled over and began pulling petulantly at the heavy diaper that bulged between her legs. Jolie reached for a dry diaper and the baby wipes. Mona lay quietly while her diaper was changed, but then she lifted both her arms and begged pitifully, "Mommy."

Jolie glanced at her wristwatch and instantly capitulated. With less than two hours to the end of business, she was getting as nervous as the proverbial cat in a room full of rocking chairs. Besides, Mona needed her mom. "Okay, come on." Hauling Mona, who was solid and heavy despite her tiny size, into her arms, Jolie struggled to her feet and carried the baby out of her own office and into the corridor. After winding their way through a maze of curtained alcoves and roughly walled halls, they entered the darkened computer room and followed the sound of tapping keys and murmurs. Dessie was hovering over Benny's shoulder.

"Yes. That's it! That's it! You got it!"

Benny slid his chair back from the console. "It's about time."

"Are we there?" Jolie asked excitedly, at the same moment that Mona spied her Mommy and sobbed with relief.

"Come here, angel girl," Dessie said, reaching up to take her daughter from Jolie. "Did you have a nice nap?"

"Are we there?" Jolie repeated her question to Benny since Dessie had switched into Mommy mode.

"Gotta get it on tape," he said. "Then we're there."

"How much longer?"

"How long we got?"

"Less than ninety minutes."

"I'll give it my best shot, but we could really use another half-hour."

Jolie closed her eyes and fisted her hands, hoping with all her might. "I'm going to call PH and see if I can wangle the extra time. You two stay with it."

She turned to go, but not before Dessie caught her by the arm. "Did John call?"

John was Dessie's ex. He was late on his child support, and Dessie had been calling and paging him for days. Jolie shook her head. "Sorry, no."

"That bum. You'd think he'd be concerned enough about his daughter to at least pay his child support on time."

Dessie lived by the skin of her teeth, barely making ends meet, as she had not had the financial cushion with which Jolie and, to a lesser extent, Benny were able to begin. With business earnings still uncertain, they weren't able to draw regular paychecks yet, and Dessie depended heavily on the child support paid by her ex.

"Dessie, let me cover John's payment this month," Jolie began, but Dessie was already stubbornly shaking her head.

"Benny's already offered, but it's not either of your places to provide for my daughter."

"She can't eat air, Dessie."

"I know that," Dessie declared, settling Mona on her ample hip. "And I won't let my daughter do without. If I have to, I'll borrow, but not until I have to."

"Okay," Jolie said. "So long as you know where to come when you have to."

"She knows," Benny said dryly, never taking his eyes off the computer screen.

"I could just strangle John Blake," Dessie muttered. "He didn't show up for his last visitation."

"Nothing unusual in that," Benny volunteered.

Jolie shook her head. She couldn't argue. The debacle of John and Dessie's short marriage had just confirmed everything her own parents' experiences had taught Jolie. She couldn't remember when her parents had been married to each other, but she remembered their fussing and fighting and their numerous other marriages well enough. At times she had felt like a bone caught between two ferocious dogs. It had been so bad that by her earliest teens Jolie had demanded to be sent to a boarding school and begun regulating visitation herself, making certain that the two never crossed paths. The arrangement had worked so well that it had freed them both to pursue their many romantic interests. As a consequence, her mother had just divorced her fourth husband and was happily hunting number five, while her father actually seemed fairly settled with his third wife in a marriage of five years' duration. Jolie figured he had another couple of years before the old seven year itch seized him. At that point, if he held true to pattern, he would very likely "trade down," as he would jokingly say, which to Jolie meant that her next stepmother was likely to be about her own age, as his wives tended to get younger and younger.

Based on that wealth of experience, Jolie couldn't for the life of her understand why anyone ever even attempted marriage. Benny, too, was divorced and had been for several years. Since he showed no interest in remarriage nor maintained contact with his ex, Jolie supposed that they were of a like mind on the matter. Dessie, on the other hand, worried Jolie. Despite her experience with John, she remained a true romantic, often saying that she'd do it all again just for Mona.

Jolie's gaze traveled to the babe, who clung trustingly to

her short, plump mother, one chubby hand clasping the thick, blond braid that hung between Dessie's shoulder blades. A pang of longing assailed Jolie, but she ruthlessly suppressed it. Marriage and motherhood were not for her. She would not trust her heart to romance, and she would never attempt what Dessie was doing, rearing a child on her own. No, she was better off as she was. The business and her friends were enough for her, and it seemed fitting that the two should be so heavily entwined.

"I'd better get on the phone to PH," she said, turning away from the console. "You two just get that tape down."

"Will do," Benny promised, while Dessie pulled a chair around and sat down with Mona in her lap.

Jolie could hear Dessie crooning to her daughter and Benny's fingers tapping a machine-gun staccato on the keyboard as she hurried away, but her thoughts had already turned to Channing Hawkins. Though she hated having to ask for more time, she realized that some part of her was eager to interact with Channing Hawkins again. Jolie was pretty good at sizing up people, but Hawkins had her stumped. He wasn't what she'd expected. Tall and thin with shaggy, sandy brown hair and bright blue eyes, his face long and narrow, he seemed an odd combination of computer nerd, with his fashionably small rectangular glasses and plain white shirt, and high school jock of the boy-next-door variety, as if he hadn't quite filled out his lanky frame yet. He was known for his business acumen, and yet he'd been amazingly approachable in person. She admitted to herself what she'd never admit to another living soul. She rather liked Channing Hawkins. He was oddly attractive in a visceral way. Somehow she thought an extra half-hour wouldn't be too tough to get.

"What do you mean it's already too late?"

Jolie got a death grip on the telephone receiver and imagined it was Fastidious Efficiency's scrawny neck.

"Didn't Mr. Hawkins tell you that he leaves the office an hour early on Fridays?" the secretary asked snidely.

Jolie felt panic well up. Had Channing Hawkins been sandbagging her, setting her up for failure, deliberately withholding important information? Jolie smacked the desk with her fist.

"I'll sue!"

"Sue?" Fastidious Efficiency screeched.

"You tell Channing Hawkins that I'll keep his butt in court for the next ten years, so help me God. This is malfeasance! He deliberately misled me!"

"You can't sue—"

"The hell I can't. One of the benefits of being a lawyer. You tell that snake in the grass—better yet, I'll tell him myself."

"Mr. Hawkins can't be disturbed right now!"

"So he *is* still there," Jolie said smugly. "You have two minutes to get him on the line. Or would you rather explain how you were responsible for instigating litigation against him?"

She could feel the other woman's consternation and fear.

"One minute forty-five seconds and counting," Jolie said firmly.

"Hold on," the secretary snapped.

Not ten seconds later, Channing Hawkins came on the line.

"Hawkins."

"You lied to me," Jolie accused hotly.

Silence. Then a very stern voice demanded, "Who is this?"

Unease shivered through Jolie; she shook it away. Hadn't that idiot secretary even told him who was on the line? "It's

Jolie Winters, and you said nothing to me about leaving the office an hour early on Fridays!"

"Jolie Winters."

She thought she heard an odd note of satisfaction in his voice, but she didn't let it deter her. "That's right, and you aren't getting out of our arrangement this easily. Not only do I expect you to be at that office in another hour, I think you owe me a little leeway. Another thirty minutes should do it."

"No can do," was the easy reply.

Jolie closed her eyes, defeat choking the air from her lungs. "Now listen, Hawkins. I happen to be an attorney. Believe me, I could make a pretty strong case—"

"You misunderstand me, Miss Winters," he interrupted. "You're quite right that I forgot to inform you that I habitually leave the office an hour early on Fridays, but I simply cannot delay my departure."

"Then you have to give me until Monday morning to deliver the proposal," she argued.

"I can't do that. I have my own deadline to work against, you know. You'll just have to bring the proposal to my house tonight."

"Your house!" Jolie collapsed back into her chair, trying to take in the ramifications of this proposal.

"Will seven o'clock be convenient?" he asked smoothly.

Seven o'clock. Jolie closed her eyes in a silent prayer of thanks. For another three hours she'd meet him in the men's room of the bus station. "S-seven o'clock will be fine."

"Excellent. Come casual. Phil doesn't like formality."

Phil? she wondered. The possible ramifications of *that* were staggering, but she let them pass unexamined, choosing instead to concentrate on taking down directions to his lakeside home.

"Seven o'clock sharp," she promised, "and I apologize for jumping to conclusions."

He chuckled. "Apology accepted."

Jolie hung up the phone a few moments later and whispered a heartfelt prayer of gratitude before flying back down to the computer room to let Dessie and Benny know that they'd just been handed a break—again. It hadn't escaped her notice that good fortune had once more come at the hands of Channing Hawkins.

Now who the heck, she wondered, was Phil? And what influence did he hold over the man who controlled her future?

Chapter Two

Jolie changed clothes twice and hoped that she wasn't so tired she'd forget some portion of the presentation. Casual had never seemed so difficult. Everything hinged on this night's work, and she felt the responsibility keenly. She'd never before given an actual presentation, though she'd sat in on a few in order to answer legal and contractual questions. Nothing of this magnitude, though. Armed with video cassette, artfully bound report and transparencies and dressed in freshly pressed khakis, white silk tank and filmy gold overshirt, her unruly hair held back by a thin band of hard, white plastic, she was ready to face the dragon.

The analogy was not far from reality if Channing Hawkins's "house" was an accurate indication. The term *mansion* did not quite apply, nor did *castle.* The latter seemed more apt, however, given the pair of white stone turrets that guarded the gate and grounds and were then repeated at the front of the house. The building was an odd mixture of elements: white stone accented with red brick in the window arches, door casement, drive and columns that supported the covered portico between the turrets flanking the impressive entry with its enormous green doors heavy with leaded glass panels. The green was repeated in the steeply sloping roof and the lush two-acre lawn. As she drove her small, economy-model car along the gently curving lane toward the house, she glimpsed flashes of the murky blue of the lake upon the banks of which the house was built. The property itself was flanked with trees and scrubby undergrowth, a shield against prying eyes, no doubt, like the brick wall that faced the street. Jolie couldn't escape the feeling that she'd entered a small private kingdom.

She parked her car beneath the portico, got out and gathered her briefcase and handbag from the back seat, still littered with a box of unpacked files and the leftovers of too many fast-food meals, then marched up the short walk to the massive front doors and looked around for a doorbell. She didn't find one, at least not one of the sort she expected. No mundane little lighted button presented itself. Instead, she had to seriously consider the large brass bell and attached ringer fixed via a heavy metal bracket to the side of the house. After first knocking, to no avail, she glanced at her wristwatch and did the only thing she could find to do, clanged that brass bell for all it was worth. Perhaps a half-minute later, one of those big green doors slowly swung inward, emitting a gust of blessedly cool air.

Jolie stared at the child in the doorway. She was perhaps eight or nine years old, a small, chubby girl with very long, ash-blond hair held back by an elastic headband, wearing enormous glasses with thick lenses. Dressed in a baggy T-shirt, shorts and slip-on tennies, she glared at Jolie owlishly.

"Come on," she said unenthusiastically. "He's expecting you."

With that, she abruptly turned and led the way across the flagstoned entry past the two turrets, which Jolie noted were nothing more than stairwells. Jolie stepped through the door, closed it behind her and followed. They walked down a wide, open hall flanked by enormous rooms filled with comfortable furnishings. Jolie took note of a large living room, a game room, a library, a formal dining room, a bar of sorts, a den and the most magnificent kitchen she'd ever seen. She tried not to gape by fixing her mind on the necessary pleasantries.

"I'm, ah, Jolie Winters."

The girl slid a look over her shoulder that clearly said, "Duh."

They walked past what could only be called a combination conference room and office, complete with executive desk and meeting table, opposite a breakfast room with an enormous aquarium built into one wall. The girl opened one of several French doors and stepped out onto a broad verandah scattered with several dining tables, one of them set for dinner, and chairs. Ceiling fans whirred overhead, reducing the temperature in the immediate area by several degrees. It was still warm enough to make Jolie yearn for the cool interior of the house, but she clutched her two bags and followed the girl across the flagstones to the steps which ran the length of the house and descended gracefully to the green grass below.

The yard sloped away to a narrow beach and a dock with two boat slips. A small white stone and red brick building with a green roof sat to one side. Brick pathways curved across the lush yard, linking the dock and outbuildings with the verandah and house. The girl stepped down onto one of those brick pathways and turned right. It was then that Jolie saw the bricked patio hedged with low shrubs and flower beds. What amounted to an outdoor kitchen had been built in the near corner, complete with a covered bar area and an enormous brick grill.

Channing Hawkins stood before the grill in cut-offs, tank top and scruffy deck shoes. Tall and lean, he looked oddly boyish with his damp, sandy hair combed back from his face. His glasses had disappeared, leaving his vibrant blue eyes unguarded. He waved a very long fork at Jolie and called, "How do you like your steak?"

Jolie stopped where she was, some distance away yet, and looked down at the girl, who turned a frown on her. "I didn't come for dinner."

The girl shrugged. "You did if Chan says you did. I'm supposed to get you something to drink. What d'you want?"

Jolie searched her mind for an appropriate response. She usually had coffee for business meetings, but as meetings went, this one was turning out to be very unbusinesslike. "Uh, what do you have?"

The girl rattled off an impressive array of beverages, everything from imported beers to specialty sodas, and ended with, "You wanna wine list?"

Cheeky little thing, Jolie thought, and for the first time she wondered who the kid belonged to. And where was this mysterious Phil? She smiled woodenly and said, "I'll just have iced tea."

"Sweet or diet?"

"Sweet."

The girl spun away and went to the bar, opening a small refrigerator hidden beneath it. She extracted a can and carried it back to Jolie. In the meantime, Channing Hawkins set aside his fork, adjusted the heat beneath the grill, wiped his hands on a kitchen towel and came forward to greet her.

"Have any trouble finding us?"

"None at all."

He glanced at the two bags clutched before her and said, "Just put those down on one of the chairs."

Reluctantly, she did as he instructed, then took her drink from the girl.

"Thanks."

The girl shrugged. It was her he addressed when next Hawkins spoke. "Honey, why don't you toss that salad now? And if the bread's cool enough, slice it."

The girl nodded and hurried away without so much as another glance in Jolie's direction.

"Now then," he said, rubbing his hands together, "about that steak. I take mine medium well. Phil likes hers rare, just warmed, I should say. So I can do anything in between. How about it?"

Jolie felt extremely awkward. "Mr. Hawkins, I—"

"Channing," he said. "We're casual around here."

But Jolie wasn't really listening. Something he'd said before had suddenly registered. "Did you say 'hers?'"

He grinned and nodded. "Yeah. She prefers Phil to Carol Ann. It's short for Phillips."

"As in Phillips Hawkins?" Jolie asked.

"That's right. Donnelly Phillips was her biological father. When he died, I adopted her."

Jolie knew part of the story. Donnelly Phillips had been an eccentric genius who had retired early from one of the big corporations, only to team up with an untested Hawkins fresh from college. Married late in life, he'd been widowed soon after, and then a few years later had died himself. Jolie hadn't realized he'd had a child or that Channing Hawkins had taken on the responsibility of that child.

"I didn't realize."

"No reason why you should. Now, back to that steak..."

Jolie shook her head. "I didn't intend to eat."

"Have you already had dinner?"

"No, but—"

"Vegetarian?"

"No."

"Then it's settled. Now tell me how you want it cooked before it's too late."

She opened her mouth to argue, then shut it again. Perhaps it was a test of sorts, and if dinner was the price for a fair hearing of the proposal, who was she to argue? Her stomach rumbled as if in agreement. "Medium well is fine."

"Ah. A woman after my own heart." He headed back toward the grill, indicating with a jerk of his head that she should follow. "Bring your drink over and take a seat on one of those bar stools."

Once more she did as instructed. When she'd settled herself beneath the awning over the bar, she took another look around while he adjusted the flames under each of the steaks again.

"You have a really beautiful place here."

"Thanks. We like it."

"Mind if I ask who designed the house?"

He turned a wide grin on her. "Phil did."

He was joking. He had to be. "Phil? That little girl?"

"Two years ago," he confirmed. "When she was seven."

He wasn't joking. She could only gape at him.

"Well, to be honest, Phil only drew up the front elevation and the floor plan, but I liked it better than anything the architects had come up with, so we went with it. Some changes had to be made, of course, to allow for structural integrity and code enforcement, and I added a few touches of my own, specifically the kitchen and a home office, but the overall design is hers. I have a framed crayon drawing of the front of the house hanging in my office."

No wonder the house made her think of fairy tales and knights in shining armor! With a little girl for a designer, what else could one expect? Jolie shook her head. "That's amazing."

"Phil's an amazing kid," Hawkins said. "She inherited Donnelly's genius. In fact, I suspect she surpasses him in sheer IQ."

Jolie said the first thing that came to mind. "It can't be easy raising a child that smart."

Hawkins shook his head easily, apparently unoffended. "Nope. Not easy at all. But to tell you the truth, I think it's harder for her than it is for me. Sometimes I wonder who's raising who, frankly. I got her when she was three, and the first night she read *me* a bedtime story."

Jolie thought of Dessie and how difficult parenting Mona was at times. She could only imagine what Channing Hawkins had dealt with, *was* dealing with.

"I'll tell you something else," he went on conversationally. "I've always known that at some point a girl would need a mother, but that point came a lot sooner with Phil than I expected. It's hard for a guy to relate to everything that a little girl gets up to, and I'm feeling more and more lost all the time. I suspect she wants to trade me in sometimes for a conventional family."

Jolie nodded, thinking about her own childhood. "I suspect that's so at some point with every child in a nontraditional family."

"You may be right," he conceded, "but Phil's a special case. Even if I could manage to give her what I had, it would take a special woman to deal with her at this stage. Phil's just not your average little girl. My mom says she's more kid than I give her credit for being, but she's never before dealt with an eight-year-old who could teach herself to read Japanese."

"Oh, my God," Jolie breathed, and Channing Hawkins nodded in agreement.

"Yep, that's about the way I see it."

The idea of such intelligence overwhelmed her. Jolie shivered, thankful she wasn't the one dealing with it. "I barely mastered Spanish," she muttered, "and if I don't keep it up, I lose big chunks of it."

"Yeah, I know what you mean," Hawkins said, chuckling. "I took French all through high school and in college and couldn't construct a decent sentence in that language now. I suppose it would come back to me in time."

"My advisor thought Spanish would be more practical for Texas," Jolie explained, and the topic of foreign languages kept them occupied until the steaks were done.

"We'll eat on the verandah," Hawkins said, forking the steaks onto a platter. "Phil will have the table laid by now."

Jolie gathered up her briefcase and purse and followed him back the way she and Phil had come earlier. The back of the house was constructed almost entirely of glass, and Jolie saw that the verandah was roofed by its second-story twin. Every room along the back of the house would have a view of the lake and the city beyond and would open onto a verandah. Very nice—and to think it had been devised by a seven-year-old. Jolie could only marvel.

Phil had, indeed, laid the table with a gorgeous salad, baked potatoes and bread fresh from one of those automatic machines. She added frosted glasses to the heavy stoneware place settings as Channing and Jolie climbed the steps. "I'm starved," Phil announced as Channing placed the steaks on the table.

"Dig in, then." He came around the table to take Jolie's bags and set them aside, then pulled out her chair for her. Phil didn't wait. She helped herself to a steak and began cutting it up.

"Perfect," she announced, forking a blood-red bite into her mouth. Jolie looked away. She'd never been fond of rare meats. Channing took his place and poured the malt liquor next to his plate into the frosted bowl of the stemmed tumbler.

"Eat up, Jolie. I can call you Jolie, can't I?"

"Of course," Jolie answered, tipping the iced tea from her can into her glass.

"Chan doesn't like to put on airs," Phil explained, her mouth full.

"Mind your manners, Phil," Chan scolded mildly. She rolled her eyes, but she sat up straight, removed her elbows from the table and began chewing with her mouth closed. Jolie looked down to hide her smile. She *was* just a kid, after all.

The steaks were excellent. Jolie was amazed at how quickly Channing made his disappear, along with everything else on his plate.

"There's another potato in the oven," Phil said as Channing buttered his third inch-thick slice of bread.

Channing's eyes immediately lit with interest, but good manners made him hesitate. "Maybe you'd care for it, Jolie?"

She looked at her half-full plate and shook her head, smiling. "Hardly. I'll do well to finish what I already have."

"Phil?"

The girl grimaced. "You know I'm going to eat just enough so you'll let me have dessert," she said.

Channing grinned at that pronouncement and said to Jolie, "Phil has a thing for sweets."

"And strawberries and ice cream are my favorite," the little girl confirmed unrepentantly.

He shoved his chair back and got up. "Anyone else want anything from the kitchen?"

Jolie and Phil both shook their heads, and he left them to fetch that second baked potato.

"He always eats like that," Phil said after a moment. "He has a really high metabolism. Probably won't put on any weight for another ten or fifteen years, but even then middle age will look good on him."

"Wish I had that problem," Jolie murmured.

Phil dropped her fork with a clank and rolled her eyes again. "You aren't going to be one of *them,* are you? One of those skinny women who obsesses about her weight? I *hate* that."

"I am not skinny," Jolie said defensively. "I'm slender." She made a face, adding, "But I have puffy thighs because I sit on my butt too much."

Phil drew back and looked down at Jolie's lap. "Maybe you should take up running," she said. "That's what Amanda does."

Jolie didn't want to know, and yet she couldn't help herself. "Amanda?"

"Chan's ex."

For some reason, Jolie felt as if she'd just had the rug pulled from beneath her, though she did her best not to show it by concentrating on her salad. "I didn't realize Channing had been married."

"Yep. Been divorced almost six years," Phil said, forking potato into her mouth. "Between you and me, I don't think he's ever really gotten over her."

Unaccountably, Jolie felt her stomach drop and her appetite flee. She turned over a piece of lettuce and swallowed. "Oh?"

Phil twirled her fork and said, "She's really beautiful, you know? Blond and blue-eyed and, like, really built. *She* didn't have puffy thighs."

Suddenly, Jolie recognized the girl's game. She laid her fork down, templed her fingers over her plate and turned a glare on the genius. "You don't have to be nasty, and for the record, my interest in Channing Hawkins is purely business. I'm not into romance."

"Don't you wanna get married?"

"No."

Phil sat back in her chair, smug with satisfaction. "Good. Cause he wouldn't look twice at you that way."

"Or anyone else, if you have anything to say about it," Jolie said baldly.

Something vulnerable flickered behind Phil's owlish eyes, but then she jutted her chin forward and declared, "Don't think you know me or what I want because you don't."

"Ditto," Jolie said. "You may be smart, but you're not clairvoyant. Otherwise, you'd know I'm after a contract with PH and nothing more."

Phil glared at her a moment longer, but then she visibly relaxed. "I just wouldn't want you to think you had a chance with him," she said, "when I know he's still got a thing for Amanda."

Amanda, Jolie thought, of the slim, firm thighs. She wasn't fooled by Phil's demeanor, however. The kid was terrified of losing Chan to someone else. That, or she was a perfect little tyrant. Either way, Jolie couldn't help feeling somewhat sorry for her. Instinct told her to approach the girl as an equal rather than the child she was. Jolie picked up her fork again.

"Maybe you could give me some tips on how to deal with Channing. I really, really want this contract."

Phil folded her legs on her chair and seemed to give it some thought. "Don't underestimate him," she said. "Chan's really smart, and he protects the company. But he has good instincts, and he'll take a chance if his gut tells him to. Just be good at whatever it is you do, and don't ever lie to him. He hates that. It's the only thing I know that makes him really mad."

Jolie nodded. "Okay. Sounds like we could work together. Thanks, Phil."

"No problem."

Channing came out of the kitchen via the breakfast room then, carrying a plate with a loaded baked potato on it. "You girls sure you don't want a share of this spud?"

"No, thanks," Jolie said.

"We're watching our figures," Phil quipped smartly, and Jolie couldn't help smiling at the kid's sheer audacity.

Chan snorted. "As if either of you has anything to worry about. Besides, Phil, you're only nine. I won't have you worrying about silly things like your figure at this age."

Phil shrugged and cut into her steak once more. "Whatever you say, Chan."

Channing feigned surprise and announced, "Oh, boy, now I'm worried. She's never this agreeable unless it suits her purpose."

Jolie glanced at Phil, a grin dancing around the corners of her mouth. She had no doubt that he was exactly right. Phil adroitly changed the subject.

"What's this business thing you two are doing?"

"Jolie has an advertising and promotional firm, and she's interested in the publicity contract for the new PC," Channing answered.

"Actually, it's not *my* company," Jolie quickly said. "I'm just one of the partners."

Her explanation of the company carried them through Channing's second potato and dessert, with Jolie describing Dessie and Benny and their functions within the partnership. After the meal, Jolie felt obligated to offer to help clean up, and was frankly surprised when Channing and Phil both readily accepted. The three of them trooped into the kitchen, laden with dirty dishes. It took only minutes to rinse the dishes, load them in the dishwasher and wipe the table and counters with an antibacterial spray that Phil produced from beneath the sink.

"Okay," Channing said, folding a damp towel after wiping down the plastic salad bowl Phil had decreed must not be put into the dishwasher, "let's see that proposal of yours."

"Can I come?" Phil asked.

Channing glanced at Jolie. "Do you mind?"

"Not at all. I'd appreciate another opinion."

"In that case, let's move into the family room," Channing said, leading the way.

"I'll just get my things," Jolie said, mentally taking a deep breath. Now that the moment had arrived, she was nervous all over again, but she wouldn't let herself feel it just yet. The future hung in the balance. She would be nervous later.

Chan watched the self-possession with which Jolie walked out of his kitchen and through the breakfast nook. She was as cool as a cucumber to the eye, but he sensed her inward turmoil. He chuckled when he thought of the way she'd handled Phil. Without the least guilt, he'd blatantly eavesdropped. Phil had surprised him with a frontal attack; she was usually more subtle about these things, but then Jolie Winters was different, and Phil knew it as well as he did. More and more, Jolie seemed to be just what he'd been looking for all this time. She'd said that she didn't want to be married, that she wasn't into romance, but that could work to his favor, too. He'd tried the romance route, and that had been a disaster. He was more interested in a calm, sensible arrangement himself. Why shouldn't marriage be as forthright and logical as business? Yes, Jolie Winters could be exactly what he was looking for.

He smiled when she returned with her bags, and led her

toward the family room with its large-screen television and state-of-the-art video system. He sat down on the butter-soft, natural tan leather couch and prepared to be impressed. Phil had claimed the ottoman, as usual. Jolie perched on the edge of the sofa next to him and brought out her bound folder.

"Given the setting, we thought this was the best format," she began, "but I have poster-size presentation mats ready for committee use."

"Let's see what you've got." He sat forward as she extracted another folder from her bag. He took that one and passed it to Phil, then scooted closer to look on with Jolie. She seemed a little uncomfortable at first, but quickly relaxed as she explained the plan of attack.

"I know the standard is to publish scholarly articles in the industry mags, but we believe that as paid advertisements, they miss the mark. No one reads them or credits them with true scientific weight precisely because they are paid advertising. Yet the message needs to get out. Our idea is to make the salient points simply and cleanly with compelling images via television, then follow that with print."

She flipped the page to reveal a color type of a glossy print. The computer was artfully pictured. Next to it in sensible, easy-to-read font was a list of capabilities. Above it in flowing script was the hook. "Swift, sleek, fiercely competent, from one of the most respected names in the business. Phillips Hawkins introduces The Hawk PC."

"I like it," Phil said, "but that logo isn't part of the design." She pointed to the shiny silhouette of the hawk in the upper-right-hand corner of the monitor.

"It's a holographic design on foil. Peel and stick. Cheap but classy. Let me show you why we think it's worth the time and effort. The video will explain."

Phil hopped up to show Jolie how to use the VCR. Chan stayed where he was and scanned the folder. Excitement was building in his chest. No small feat, considering how many of these campaigns he'd been through. This was special, though. The Hawk was his baby, his design through and through. Why hadn't he thought of that moniker himself? Hawkins yields the Hawk. He skimmed the folder. Reading quickly and with great comprehension was one of his own gifts, and he liked everything he saw. It was slick; it was effective; it was classy; it was catchy. It was right. But as he glimpsed Jolie dealing with a bossy Phil, he reminded himself that he had more at stake here than an advertising campaign. Best play his cards close to the vest for a while.

Jolie got the video set up and took the remote in hand. Phil would have done the honors herself, but Jolie was having none of it. Firmly in control, she went into prime business mode.

"Bear in mind that the voice-over is not to point. We recommend a recognizable voice with star power. Yes, it's expensive, but I think you'll see why we feel this is the right approach. Also, we were undecided about background music. We've narrowed the choice to three instrumentals, all original. Each fits beautifully with the sound effects, but we'd prefer that you make the final decision there. For purposes of presentation only, we're using a pseudo-Celtic piece called, 'In Flight'."

With that she stepped aside, aimed the remote control, and started the video.

A blank screen. The call of a bird, a hawk presumably. A sun-washed meadow and the shadow of a bird in flight, a magnificent bird, a predator. Closer and closer the shadow comes until suddenly it's as if the camera has been plucked off the meadow floor and is sailing aloft with the bird. Wind rustles by. The sunlight is blinding in spots, as if one is widely spiraling. The meadow and all its beauty shows from afar. Then the shadow of the hawk is silvered by its own shadow. As if pulled through a vortex, the camera view widens, shifts, narrows again, and as the camera zooms out, the shadow of the hawk is revealed in outline on the corner of the computer, the meadow beyond as seen through a window. The voiceover is dramatic and concise, spelling out all the essentials and hitting all the right buttons. The final screen comes up to utter silence, then, "Phillips Hawkins presents The Hawk," with the price written plainly in small letters below. The cry of the bird once more, and it is over. Twenty-two seconds of sheer magic.

Chan was breathless. Not so, Phil.

"Whoever came up with that is brilliant!" she declared, launching to her feet and waving her arms in youthful enthusiasm. "It's perfect!"

Jolie beamed at the girl. "Dessie and Ben get all the creative credit," she said. "That's Dessie in the voiceover."

"You have got the perfect partners," Phil exclaimed. "Bet you're as good on your end. Genius attracts genius, you know."

Jolie laughed and clasped both of Phil's hands in hers. Chan watched, entranced, as the two did a kind of victory dance around his ottoman, so caught up in the sheer amazement of the moment that all barriers had been momentarily lowered. Phil collapsed onto the ottoman again, and turned to him expectantly. Jolie seemed to remember that she still had selling to do.

Hurrying back to the sofa, she plopped down next to Chan and tossed pages until she got to the cost breakdown. "Now as you can see, we've worked several scenarios." She started naming famous actors with famous voices. Chan could not even concentrate. Elation had built inside him to the bursting point.

He'd felt this way once before when a short, plump, near-sighted man with more hair than presence had quietly entered his workshop at the back of your standard computer fix-it shop and matter-of-factly told him that his component design showed great promise. Chan hadn't even been aware of whose computer he'd been working on. He'd been stunned to find Donnelly Phillips standing there with one of his modified motherboards in hand, and within moments of beginning to converse with that brilliant gentleman as an equal, Chan had felt his life tilt on its axis. Great things had come from that encounter. He had the feeling that he would be looking back on *this* moment in the same way one day.

Oddly, though, his senses seemed to have gone into overdrive. The last time the experience had been cerebral. This time it was strongly physical. The warmth of Jolie's long thigh against his was enveloping. He smelled the subtle fragrance of her perfume and the clean, alcoholic residue of hair spray, the slight musk of her deodorant and beneath it all the warm redolence of woman. He'd almost forgotten that smell, the sexual power of it. His body reminded him, forcefully, that cool intellect could not completely override the primal urgencies. And his elation built.

Yes. His instincts were true. Jolie Winters was going to get her contract and more, much more. It was all he could do to keep from rubbing his hands together in male glee. She didn't know it yet, but Jolie Winters had met her match. And so had Phil.

Chapter Three

He promised that he'd have a decision for her by 10:30 Monday morning. By 10:10, Jolie was sitting in that uncomfortable chair, smiling slyly every time Fastidiously Efficient Phoebe failed to ignore her. At 10:20, the door to his office opened, and Channing Hawkins himself waved her inside. Jolie turned a smug nod in Phoebe's direction as she gracefully stood, gathered her briefcase and strolled toward that open office door. Inside, her heart was slamming double-time against the walls of her chest. She'd been chanting a silent prayer all morning. Please God. Oh, please, oh, please, oh, please, give us that contract.

She smiled confidently at Channing as she strode past him, feeling a new and unwanted appreciation for the slender, ropy body hidden beneath pleated chinos and a baggy dress shirt with rolled-back sleeves. His tie was at half-mast already, and he had pushed his glasses up onto the top of his head. His sand-brown hair had been combed straight back and left to feather untidily across his collar. He gestured at another man in the room, a blocky character who looked as though he'd just stepped out of the boxing ring, his broad nose slightly flattened, colorless hair buzzed into a flat top. He wore a surprisingly sheepish expression as Channing introduced them.

"Jolie Winters of Austin 3, I'd like you to meet Dale Bucks, Vice President of Marketing."

The two shook hands, and Bucks spoke up. "Ms. Winters, I owe you an apology."

"Oh?" she quipped, intending to put him at ease. "Did you personally tell your people not to consider Austin 3?"

He cleared his throat uncomfortably, and Jolie saw instantly that she'd hit the proverbial nail squarely on the head. "It's been my experience," he mumbled, "that a campaign of this magnitude requires the stewardship of a major player in the market."

"What Dale failed to consider," Channing said, perching on the corner of his desk, "is how advances in *technology* have made it possible for a small firm like Austin 3 to produce materials that were once labor-intensive."

Jolie didn't feel it necessary to point out that said technology was precisely the business of Phillips Hawkins Computers. From the look on Bucks's face, that point had already been made. Whether that meant good or ill for Austin 3 Jolie couldn't know.

"We've a lot of ground to cover and much to do along the way," Channing said briskly, "so let's not butt heads about what's past." He looked at Jolie and announced flatly, "You've got the contract. Now let's get your people together with Dale and our people and get busy selling computers."

Jolie thought her legs would buckle. She wasn't quite sure she could trust her ears. "We got the contract?"

"Lock, stock and barrel."

Jolie's mind reeled. She barely registered what Bucks was saying.

"My people are looking over the contract you left with Chan now. I expect we'll want a few changes, but nothing we can't come to terms with. No reason we can't start nailing down the campaign. If you'll just get your people in here, we'll get to work, ah, today preferably."

Jolie was nodding dumbly, but then she abruptly began to shake her head as reality intruded. "No, uh, you'll have to go to them. Dessie, she's our art director, brings her baby to the office, where we, um, have facilities for her."

Bucks traded looks with Channing, who shrugged and said, "One of the perks of using local talent is that you won't have to book flights and hotels."

"I'll get the process moving," Bucks said resignedly, striding toward the door. "You better call and warn your folks we're coming," he said to Jolie. She could just imagine the panic that would ensue. Benny was going to get stuck with cleaning the toilets again, poor man. It was then that the euphoria began to fill her. They'd won the contract! They were about to put their upstart little agency on the advertising map! She searched blindly for the murderous chair and dropped into it, trying to cudgel her stunned brain into working order.

"Oh, by the way," Bucks said, pausing in the open doorway, "the concept is sheer genius. My hat's off to you and your firm, Ms. Winters. Sheer genius."

Jolie nodded and then sputtered laughter as the door closed behind him.

"You were expecting failure?" Channing asked, folding his arms.

She shook her head. "No, but I was prepared to fight tooth and nail."

He shoved off the corner of his desk and walked around

behind it to plop into his chair, saying, "Dale's hardheaded and set in his ways, but he's not stupid. He knows magic when he sees it."

"Do you really think it's that good?" she asked eagerly, sliding to the very edge of her chair.

He linked his hands atop his desk blotter, fingers interwoven. "I think we're going to sell shiploads of computers, Jolie. That's what I think."

"My partners will be thrilled."

"Partners," he said, folding his forearms against the blotter. "That's precisely what I want to speak to you about now."

Jolie felt suddenly on the alert, like a wary animal in that moment of atmospheric change before an unexpected storm. But that was nonsensical. They'd already won the contract. What was there to fear? "All right."

"First, though, you'd better make that call." He waved at the phone on his desk. "Third button's an outside line."

"Oh, right." She got up from her chair and punched the button, leaning awkwardly over his desk. He shoved the phone closer to the edge and leaned back in his chair, one foot drawn up into the seat. Jolie perched on the edge of his desk and carried on a one-sided conversation that consisted of lots of low-key murmurings on her part and squeals of delight punctuated by crowing huzzahs in the background on the other end. Finally, she felt that she'd adequately prepared her partners for what was about to happen—as adequately as she could prepare them—and turned back to Channing Hawkins. She hung up the phone with a smile and wondered what she was still doing here when she could be helping Ben scrub toilets in preparation for the descent of the PH marketing staff on their humble offices. Standing, Jolie spread both hands.

"I can't thank you enough, Chan, er...I can't thank you enough. You won't be disappointed, I promise you."

"I don't expect to be," he said smoothly. "Now, about that partnership..."

She made an attempt to skirt whatever was coming. "I already have two partners and—"

"That's business," he said with a dismissive wave of one hand. "I'm talking about a *personal* partnership."

Jolie frowned. She was floundering. "I—I don't understand."

"I'm proposing a partnership," he said steadily, "between the two of us, you and me, a personal, domestic partnership, and I'm prepared to be very generous."

Jolie blinked. "I..." She didn't know what to say to that unexpected announcement. Personal? Domestic? Was this some kind of an end run? She blinked again and shook her head. "My partnership agreement with Ben and Dessie is ironclad. I should know, I drew it up myself."

He leaned back in his chair and templed his fingers. "I'm not making myself understood. Let me come at this from another direction." He studied her a moment and then asked abruptly, "What do you think of Phil?"

She felt as if she'd blundered into a deep pool well over her head. "Phil?"

"Do you like her?" he asked bluntly.

She searched hard for an honest answer. "Uh, I hadn't thought about it, really. I can't help experiencing a certain affinity with her. She's, well, growing up too fast."

He cocked his head, as if hearing more than she'd intended to reveal. "Is that how it was with you, Jolie?" he asked softly. "Did you grow up too fast?"

She shrugged, emotionally flailing, trying desperately to get her mental feet beneath her. "I, um, didn't have much choice," she muttered, adding, "My parents were, ah, somewhat irresponsible. One of us had to be adult enough to control matters."

"And that responsibility fell to you." He nodded, as if that explained a lot, though she couldn't imagine what. Sighing, he spread his hands. "I'd do anything to stop it in Phil's case. The problem is that she *knows* things. She reads them or divines them, figures them out. And once you know something, that's that. I sometimes think I have an inkling how God felt when Adam and Eve ate that damned apple."

"That bad?" Jolie asked sympathetically, more comfortable now that they weren't talking about her.

"She's upset with me because I'm making her go to middle school again next year," he revealed.

"Middle school?" Jolie echoed, certain she'd misunderstood.

He nodded absently and went on. "Even high school would probably bore her to tears, but I just can't get my mind around college yet, though I might let her try some classes at the community college this summer."

"But she's nine!" Jolie exploded.

He pointed an emphatic index finger. "Exactly. Only she doesn't *think* like a nine-year-old. I sometimes wonder if she even *feels* like a nine-year-old." He shook his head. "Don't get me wrong. I wouldn't change her for the world. The thing is, she's not only smarter than your average genius, she's stubborn, too." He spread his hands in a gesture of helplessness. "Don't ask me where she gets it. Neither of her natural parents were particularly strong personalities, but Phil is steel to the core."

"I sensed that," Jolie murmured.

"But back to us," he said, waving a hand.

Jolie coughed, floundering again. "Us?" she squeaked.

"Our partnership."

This time she was quite certain that she had missed something. "I don't understand. I've already explained that—"

He gusted a sigh of great impatience and rocked his chair forward, dropping his foot. "Will you please sit down and let me make my case."

"Your case?" she asked dumbly.

"The day you forced yourself in here, I let you make your case, didn't I? Now it's my turn. You owe me that much, don't you think?"

She gaped at him for a full half-minute. "I don't know what you're talking about!"

He rose slowly from his chair. "I'm trying to tell you, aren't I? Now, why don't you just sit down and listen?"

She glanced at the torture rack he called a chair and grimaced inwardly. Apparently, parking her behind in that nasty thing was the only way she was going to find out what he was trying to say. She was just about to lower herself into it when he muttered something unintelligible, shot around the desk, grasped her by the shoulders and guided her back the way he'd come. After pushing her down into his comfy desk chair, he leaned back against the edge of the desk itself and drew up one foot to hang his heel on a lower drawer handle.

"Okay," he said, "we've already established that Phil needs a mother."

Jolie flopped back in his chair. "We have?"

He gave her a quelling look, as if to say that he didn't appreciate pretense. "We discussed it first on Friday, and I was making the point again just now."

"You were?"

He frowned, positively glowered. "Are you going to hear me out or not?"

"Gladly," she snapped. "If you'll just get to the point."

"Fine. I want you to marry me. There, that's the point."

Jolie sank down in his chair, mouth gaping, expecting laughter or confetti showers, anything to signal that it was some kind of joke. He just stared at her impatiently, as serious as death. Had she stumbled into an alternate universe?

"I, ub, murgy you?" she gurgled at him.

"It's a perfectly reasonable plan," he said lightly. "Mutually beneficial, I might add. You fit my criteria to a T. You're smart, savvy, strong-willed. You have empathy with Phil, and you like her. Moreover, you've got gumption, Jolie Winters, and passion. Oh, and you didn't let her snow you. I heard that little exchange at the table the other night, you know, all that guff about me still being in love with Amanda. You didn't buy a word of it, to your credit. Amanda was the wrong woman, even if she does have thinner thighs."

Ow. Jolie was on her feet and yelling before she even realized he'd hit the nerve. "My thighs are just fine!"

He lifted a brow in surprise, then pointedly looked down at the short, slender skirt of her melon-orange suit. "Yes, they are. Exceptional, actually."

Exceptional? She looked down at herself. He thought her thighs were exceptional? Lifting her gaze, she narrowed her eyes at him.

He smiled then, a butter-wouldn't-melt-in-his-mouth smile, and added, "As I said, you're perfect for the position."

The wonder evaporated in the sheer effrontery of that ludicrous statement. She punched her fists into the tops of her hips, demanding, "Is this how you ask a woman to marry you? 'You're perfect for the position,'" she mimicked. "The position! You call this...this *interview* a marriage proposal?"

"Why not?" he asked most reasonably. "You said yourself that you wanted no part of romance."

"When did I say that?"

"Friday night, talking to Phil."

Okay, so she'd said it. "That's beside the point," she huffed.

"That's the *whole* point," he said. "And it's a wise decision on your part. I can attest to it, having been down that road myself. These things need to be approached sensibly, straight on. A man and a woman should know what they're getting into when they marry. Spell it out in black and white, I say, none of this starry-eyed nonsense. It's bound to backfire."

Jolie fought the urge to slowly back away as if he were a rabid dog. This man was dangerous. He was making entirely too much sense! She was actually starting to listen—and consider. And why shouldn't she? Hadn't she said or thought these very things at times? Marriage was not something that ought to be entered into amid the fog of romantic emotions. Marriage was... Marriage! Holy cow, the man was talking marriage! To her! She licked her lips, trying to find reasonable arguments against so unreasonable an approach. "I—I don't think you've thought this through. I'm not really your t-type."

He waved her rebuttal away. "Nonsense. You're exactly my type. I like everything about you, the way you handle yourself, the way you meet challenges, that sauciness and pride, your smarts and determination. Your looks. I'm a sucker for tall, willowy, freckled redheads. With slender thighs."

Warmth flushed through her. She grappled against it. "Th-that's all very well, but *you're* not *my* type!"

"Oh? And what would your type be?"

She opened her mouth—and closed it. Mentally, she ticked off the list. Intelligent. Honest. Generous. Responsible. Decisive. Compassionate. Determined. Attractive. Independent. Sensible. She gulped, unable to think of a single attribute that he did not seem to possess in spades. She chose another argument. ''W-we have nothing in common.''

He chuckled. ''Oh, come on. We're business people, movers and shakers, you and I, and we go after what we want with hammer and tongs. We play the game, but we play by our own rules. For instance, I never wear a suit.'' He leaned forward, nose to nose with her and went on silkily, ''You never wear nylons.'' He folded his arms. ''But we both manage to present the business image. I'll tell you something else about us. We're not greedy, but we take what we need and leave the rest for the other guy, with no apologies.''

''You don't know what you're talking about,'' she told him with no small measure of alarm.

''Don't I? Tell me you believed me when I said I'd forgotten that I leave the office early on Fridays.''

She wanted to, but he would know she lied. She'd believed everything but that. Hadn't she silently accused him of sandbagging? His smirk made her want to slap him. Instead she folded her arms.

''I schemed to get you to my house so I could observe you with Phil,'' he admitted shamelessly. ''You went along because it gave you what you wanted, time and a chance to make your pitch. And you did it without complaining, just as I would have.''

''Only because it was worth it,'' she grumbled.

He spread his hands as if to say she'd made his point for him. ''Now consider,'' he said, ''your company's on its way. When this campaign hits the airwaves a few months from now, doors will be opening all over the country. But you won't have the wherewithal to take the top offers because you sold yourself short on this contract, not that I'd have done any differently, mind you. Nevertheless, you could use a healthy infusion of working capital. Marry me, and I'll provide it. Then there is the power of the Hawkins name. The doors the campaign won't open, the name will. With my influence and backing and your savvy, you can take your little three-man company straight to the top in record time. Add to that the home and all else we'll share—the companionship, vacations, income, goals... What more could you ask?"

What more, indeed? He made a heck of a case, and yet, some part of her was smarting sharply. She couldn't imagine why. He was right that a simple business deal made more sense than the maudlin, messy, roller-coaster affairs that her parents called marriage. And yet, some part of her grieved the lack of...what? Love? She swallowed a thick lump in her throat.

"Okay, we know what I get out of this arrangement. What do you get?"

"A wife," he said simply. "A helpmate, a partner and a mother for my daughter. If you take me, you take Phil. That's non-negotiable. Marry me, adopt her. Period."

She shook her head, feeling absurdly close to tears for no explainable reason. "That's absurd. Marriage is more than that. Or it should be."

"Oh, I agree," he said in a voice gone suddenly husky. "Do you think I'd make this proposal if I didn't think we could have *that,* too."

She wrinkled her brow at him. "What are you saying?"

He smiled slightly, and something warm and liquid pooled inside her. "This requires demonstration," he said, reaching out a hand to slide it around the curve of her waist.

Realization dawned. She staggered as he drew her to him. "Oh, no."

He pulled her into the V of his legs, sliding his free hand

around the nape of her neck. "Oh, yes," he whispered, angling his head to fit his mouth to hers.

The first shock of it sent her reeling. Without the twin anchors of his hands, she suspected that she'd have spun away into infinity. But then he slowly straightened away from the edge of the desk, wrapping his arms around her and bending her head back as he gained his full height. Suddenly she was very much *there,* very much aware of everything that he was doing. He took a small step forward, pressing himself against her. Had she thought him slender? He felt as solid as a block wall, as hard as granite, but warm, *hot* even, positively steaming, and alarmingly, seductively male.

When he slid his tongue into her mouth, she lifted her hands to his shoulders and grabbed on. When had she closed her eyes? Why did his tongue feel so terribly *intimate* inside her mouth? More important, why didn't she pull away, put a stop to this insanity?

It was as if she had no control over her own body, as if she could not quite talk herself out of this experience. When her arms slid around his neck, she moaned in despair, knowing she was lost to all sensibility. He made as thorough a job of that kiss as she knew that he did everything else, exploring every cranny of her mouth, fitting her body to his so perfectly that she began to wonder where he left off and she began. When he slid his hands down to cup her buttocks and pull her hard against his rocking pelvis, she exploded in screaming shards of desire and sheer terror in equal measures. She pinwheeled away from him, gasping, and came to rest against the computer desk behind her. She couldn't tell which of them was more surprised.

They stared at each other until Phoebe thrust open the door. Channing was the first to recover. Calmly, he looked over his shoulder.

"Ms. Winters tripped," he lied smoothly. Turning back to her, he surveyed her with blatant intent. He had proven his point; he intended to prove it again, as often as circumstance permitted. "Are you all right?" he asked, allowing his tone to drop once more into that husky range that made the tiny hairs lift on her arms.

Jolie cleared her throat and gingerly stepped away from the computer. "Yes. Fine. Thank you. Foolish of me, tripping like that." She tried a smile, then abandoned the effort, unable to quite make her gaze meet his or his too-alert secretary's.

"That'll be all, Phoebe," he said. Phoebe pursed her mouth but didn't move so much as another muscle until he repeated himself, sternly this time. "That will be all." Reluctantly, the secretary backed out and closed the door.

Jolie wondered unkindly if the woman was listening at the keyhole—except the lock was electronic, no keyhole required. "If that woman was my secretary, I'd fire her," she muttered darkly.

Channing lifted a hand to the back of his neck, sinking down on the edge of his desk again. "Yeah, well, you have to understand about her. Phoebe was Donnelly's secretary. She was fiercely protective of him, fiercely loyal. Everyone knew she was in love with him. When he married Phil's mother, Phoebe was crushed. That's when Donnelly asked me to take her on. When Donnelly's wife died, she grieved for him and would have comforted him if he'd allowed it. Then when he fell ill, she took care of him. I don't think she quite knows how to live with him gone, frankly, and so, if she's unpleasant, well, hell, I figure she's entitled."

Jolie's mouth thinned regretfully. She was sorry she'd brought it up. Now she had to add kindhearted and patient to his list of attributes, not to mention sexy as all get-out. She wanted to run and hide before that list got any longer.

"I, um, have to go," she mumbled, widely skirting the desk where he perched, studying her. He said nothing as she grabbed up her briefcase and turned toward the door, but then, as she reached for the knob, his next statement froze her in place.

"Naturally you'll want to think over what we've discussed this morning," he said reasonably. "But don't think too long."

Was that the hint of a threat? She whirled around. "What's that supposed to mean?"

He chuckled as he eased down into his chair. "It means I'm thirty-six and not getting any younger."

"Oh."

"I'll be here until seven this evening," he said as she turned once more for the door. "Phil has music lessons."

She wrapped her hand around the doorknob and turned.

"My patience does have limits," he said as she pulled the door open.

"So does mine," she muttered as she stalked through the door. She was in the elevator on her way down before it occurred to her that she had not actually refused him. The man had asked her to marry him after an acquaintance of mere days, and she hadn't actually said no. She ran to her car in the parking lot, and she was still running when she entered her own office across town and slammed the door.

"What do you mean he asked you to marry him?"

Jolie threw out her arms and addressed Dessie. "Just that. He made it sound like a business deal, a partnership, but he was talking about *marriage.*"

"To you?" Benny clarified. "Hoo, boy, the guy must be crazy."

Dessie shot Benny a murderous glare and swung her foot sideways, kicking his shin. "Ow." He frowned at her from around Mona's plump middle; she was standing in his lap and trying to climb onto his shoulders. Dessie and Ben sat in matching chairs—comfortable if scruffy chairs—in front of Jolie's desk, before which Jolie paced. Mona had been passed between the two a number of times while Jolie agitatedly explained what had transpired between her and Channing Hawkins earlier in the day. Well, not exactly *all* that had transpired. A fairly heavily edited version, in fact. What point in bringing up that kiss? Not to mention the way he'd curled her toes with it.

Jolie let the insult pass. Ben was a dear and trusted friend, but she was no more convinced of his marriageability than he was of hers. Ben was like a big, clumsy puppy that growled a lot but more often than not wound up biting his own tail.

"I just don't get it," she said. "He seems like such a logical man, but to propose marriage like that, out of the blue." She shook her head. "He implied that I have until tonight to make up my mind. 'Til seven, he said."

Dessie exchanged a look with Benny, who turned Mona and actually sat her down in his lap. "What if you say no?" she asked tentatively.

Jolie scowled. "Well, of course I'll say no. Rather, I *have* said no. Sort of. I mean, I implied it, anyway."

Dessie sat forward in her chair. "But did he accept that? *Will* he accept it?"

"He has no choice," Jolie retorted, but the look Benny suddenly turned on Dessie seemed to say otherwise.

"We haven't inked that contract yet," he said suggestively.

"Did he threaten to pull the contract if you turned down

his marriage proposal?'' Dessie asked, going straight to the point.

Jolie stopped in her tracks and frowned at them both. ''You don't think.... He didn't say it.'' But it could be inferred.

''We haven't signed the contract yet,'' Benny said needlessly.

''And we're supposed to first thing tomorrow morning,'' Dessie pointed out. ''If he gave you until tonight to decide, then it stands to reason....'' She let the thought hang there, glancing worriedly at Ben.

Jolie threw out both arms and began to pace again, propelled by righteous anger. ''That's...that's...it's blackmail! It's sexual harassment!'' She marched around the desk, grabbing at keys and pocketbooks. ''I'll sue the computers off that overgrown geek!''

Benny plopped Mona in Dessie's lap and jumped up, intercepting Jolie on her way to the door. ''Now let's not do anything rash,'' he said placatingly. ''We don't know that's what he intends.''

''What he intends and what's happening are two very different things!'' she exclaimed. ''How dare he ask me to marry him?''

''That's just it,'' Benny argued hurriedly. ''He asked you to marry him. He didn't ask you to sleep with him. Technically, I'm not sure a marriage proposal qualifies as sexual harassment. And I don't think you should sue him until we ink that contract!''

Jolie glared hot enough to sizzle his ears. ''It's still blackmail,'' she insisted.

''Or,'' Dessie offered meekly, ''he could really want to marry you.'' Benny's brows shot into his hairline, and Dessie snapped, ''Well, he could.''

Benny wisely made no comments along that line.

"Maybe you ought to just think about it for a while," he cajoled. "You can always say you didn't understand that he wanted an answer tonight."

"Or you could agree," Dessie said hopefully. "You could always change your mind later."

"After the check clears," Benny added.

Jolie gaped at the two of them. Surely they didn't expect her to submit to this type of coercion—if that's what it was. Surely they did.

"Look," Dessie said frankly, "it's a lot to ask. But Phillips Hawkins is our shot at the big time. For me, it's the difference between paying my bills on time every month or following my ex around begging for change to feed my kid. We need this, Jo. Not just Mona and me. All of us. We need this. Can't you just, like, string him along for a few days?"

"You can sue the computers off him later," Benny pointed out hopefully. "Or, if you like, I'll just go over and punch his lights out."

"Once the deal is done," Dessie said.

Jolie sighed, knowing she very probably held all their futures in her hands—hands she'd like to see around Channing Hawkins's throat at the moment. *"We play the game, but we play by our own rules,"* he had said. *"We take what we need and leave the rest for the other guy."* Well, the sorry hound had bitten off more than he could chew this time. The gall of the man! Trying to blackmail her into mothering his child. Obviously he was too busy to bother with the girl, too cold-blooded to be a proper father, and his solution to the problem was to get himself a glorified nanny by any means necessary.

Unfortunately Dessie and Ben were right. Channing Hawkins definitely had the upper hand—for now. The real surprise was how much this new insight hurt.

"You won't need to punch his lights out," she told

Benny through clenched teeth. "I'll save that pleasure for myself. Just as soon as the deal is done."

Both Benny and Dessie wilted with relief.

"Meanwhile," Dessie began.

"Meanwhile," Jolie finished for her reluctantly, "I'd better see what I can do to make Channing Hawkins think I'm looking favorably on his proposal."

"Atta girl," Benny said approvingly, clapping her on the shoulder as if she were the center on the football team. Jolie rocked to the side and resisted the urge to rub her arm where Ben had smacked her. She hurt far worse in other places. Just what those places were, she couldn't quite put her finger on.

"If I pull this off," she said glumly, "I want you to know, you both owe me. Majorly."

"Absolutely," Dessie said. "Isn't that right, Benny?"

"Huh? Oh. Yeah. Right. Majorly." He scratched his chin, obviously mulling over something important. "On the other hand, what if you come to like the idea and actually marry the guy? Then you'd owe us. Right, Des? I mean, if she actually wound up Mrs. Channing Megabucks Hawkins, she'd sort of owe it all..." Jolie's withering stare finally made itself felt, and he let the thought drift away into befitting obscurity.

"The day I marry Channing Hawkins," she declared, enunciating each word precisely, "Satan will get frostbite on his pointy ears! You are as likely to marry—" she searched for a female equally preposterous as a match for her foolish partner and came up only with the obvious, and so she finished gamely, "—Dessie!"

Whirling, she made her exit, intent on performing the nasty deed assigned her—and completely missed the exchange of sheepish, guilty looks that took place in her wake.

Chapter Four

His palms were sweaty. How ironic was that? He hadn't felt the least qualm when making his proposal nor when formulating it. Why should he? He'd been searching a long time for just the right woman, and he had little doubt that Jolie Winters was the one. For one thing, he knew what he wanted, and for another his instincts with people were finely honed. Also, he'd had her investigated thoroughly, beginning the morning she'd burst into his office. These things were never as clean as one might hope, however.

Dealing with people lacked the clinical precision of computer technology. Perhaps that was why he was on edge. It had nothing to do with her failure to accept his proposal immediately, despite its obvious logic. He'd been prepared for that. What he hadn't been prepared for was the difficulty of waiting for her to provide him an answer. If he'd realized it was going to be this difficult, he'd have put together a different program, one designed to ameliorate the negatives of waiting for response. From sheer habit, a number of options flitted through his mind, but he gave them short shrift, having no inclination for wasting time or energy on useless hindsight.

Given the unanticipated state of his nerves, one might have expected Chan to feel great relief when the door to his office opened and Jolie Winters walked through it. Unfortunately, she had not quite got her game face in place, and in that first instant she looked fierce enough to eat glass. He knew then, without a doubt, that she meant to refuse him. Disappointment, raw and acrid, brought a foul taste to his mouth. He swallowed it down, replacing it with the same resolve that had put him on top of the heap in the business world. Those previously dismissed options began running through his mind again, despite the mask of friendly reserve that fell over Jolie's expressive face.

He'd have to warn her about that one day. A good poker face was essential to successful business negotiation. He wore his habitually, and he'd never been so glad as now. He glanced at his watch as calmly as if he hadn't been doing so every five minutes since lunch, leaned back in his chair and offered her a smile.

"You're early. I expected you to keep me waiting until the very last moment."

Jolie bypassed the chair and walked right around to slide a hip onto the end of his desk, placing her small handbag on the blotter. As she leaned toward him, his pulse jumped several beats faster, but he carefully kept that reaction to himself.

"We both know that would be pointless," she said, the silkiness of her voice making him want to drag her off the desk and into his lap, even knowing that it was false. He widened his smile and upped the ante.

"I prefer a quick wedding, something small and intimate, nothing ostentatious, say next week."

Alarm flashed behind her pale bronze eyes, but she tamed

it immediately with an affable, easy manner. "You don't know what you're asking. My parents are never available at less than a month's notice. Besides," she added coyly, "I haven't given you my answer yet."

And she wasn't going to. He saw that clearly enough. The question was, why? He decided it was to his benefit to know the answer right away. He pushed his chair back.

"Never try to bluff a bluffer, Jolie. What's going on?"

She attempted to deny it, but then the emotion he'd glimpsed when she'd entered the room burst upon her face. He was surprised to find that it was anger.

"What kind of man has to go to such lengths to coerce a woman to marry him?" she asked in a low, trembling voice.

He cocked his head, wanting to get every nuance of every word. When the salient one presented itself, he repeated it. "Coerce? What coercion have I used?"

She snorted inelegantly, her pale eyes flashing. He found he quite enjoyed the incensed Jolie. "As if you didn't know. As if it wasn't obvious."

Obvious. He had to think that over. Eventually he came up with only one rather incredible—and distasteful—possibility. "Are you suggesting that the advertising contract is somehow tied to *us?*"

"Isn't it?" she demanded, hopping off his desk and rounding on him. "I don't know why I didn't realize it myself. My partners saw it immediately."

He almost smiled at that, not because of what she accused him of, but because she hadn't come up with it on her own, which meant that her instincts had told her otherwise; she just didn't know it yet.

"Your partners are even more imaginative than I gave them credit for," he said mildly, not expecting this to convince her, as it did not.

"So you say, but what other explanation could there be, really?" She huffed, folding her arms. "You had to have a woman over whom you wield some leverage, someone you could force to do what you want."

"If that were so," he answered lazily, "I'd be married already."

She frowned, clearly not wanting to believe him.

Partly exasperated and partly amused, he flung out his arms. "Look around you, Jolie. This is a big company. I have dealings with dozens of subcontractors and hundreds of employees. If any woman who wandered into my sphere of influence would do, I'd have been married these past two years."

"Then why pick me?" she demanded, as petulant as any child.

He shook his head. "You're the only woman in all that time who meets my criteria. You're the only one I want."

She literally scoffed. "Oh, please. I'm not a complete idiot, you know. I meet your so-called criteria, whatever it really is, *and* you just happen to hold leverage over me. Very convenient."

Very *inconvenient* at the moment. But suddenly he understood the problem. As incredible as it seemed, Jolie Winters had no notion of her power as a woman. Oh, she was confident in the business arena, confident in her skills and acumen, but on a personal basis, on a sexual level, she was little girl lost. No doubt that explained her lack of romantic entanglement.

His investigators had uncovered just one semi-serious relationship in college, after which she and her acknowledged boyfriend had amicably parted. During law school, she had not even dated, which was understandable considering the stress inherent in that institution. Since then she had indulged in just one liaison, which had ended badly, with her erstwhile suitor spreading tales about her being frigid. The truth appeared to be that the man had attempted to ingratiate himself with her in an effort to learn the details of a contract she had been negotiating for the corporation that had employed her at that time. She obviously had not responded positively to his romantic blandishments, and he had not got the information he had sought. Chan admired that about her, but he understood now that it was more than strength of character on her part, and that presented him with a new problem.

How did he show her the feminine power she wielded without awakening the need to conquer with it? The last thing he wanted to do was send her out to test that power on other males. He needed time, time to think and formulate a plan of attack, time to put that plan into action. And she had unwittingly handed him the means to get it. Perhaps it wasn't the smartest decision business-wise, but it wasn't terribly foolish, either, and the outcome could be extremely rewarding personally.

He reached for a thick folder on his desk. Dale Bucks had dropped it off on his way out of the building an hour or so earlier. Flipping open the folder, Channing found what he wanted, extracted it and laid it on the corner of the desk, facing Jolie.

"That's your original contract. It's your work, your proposal. Dale assures me that the changes made by our attorneys were minor but important. I'll make you a deal right now. I sign the original. You give me ninety days to convince you that marrying me is the right thing to do."

Her eyes widened almost comically. "You aren't serious?"

He pulled out the center drawer, picked out a pen, twisted the barrel to move down the point and pulled the contract toward him. "All I need is your word and ninety days."

She tilted her head, clearly puzzled. "How do you know you can trust me?"

He shrugged. "If I can't trust you, I shouldn't marry you, should I?"

She bit her lip, watching as he flipped through the pages to the signature line. He poised the pen and turned a silent question at her, one brow arched. She hugged herself. "This is crazy."

"I believe I can change your mind about that if you'll give me a chance."

"You don't know me as well as you think you do if you believe that," she retorted.

"Ninety days will give us both time to get to know each other as we should."

She stared at the contract and said, "I'll want definite parameters spelled out—what you expect of me, what I can expect of you."

Gotcha! he thought. He said, "I'm sure we can come to terms." Swiftly, he penned his name, laid the pen across the contract and shoved the whole toward her.

She approached the desk and the contract like a wary animal expecting a trap to spring at any moment. He silently watched the war that she waged within herself.

"Ninety days," he prodded evenly. "Three months. That's all I'm asking."

After a moment, she carefully picked up the pen. An instant later she bent over the desk and signed her name with a flourish on the correct line. She tossed the pen down and backed away.

"It won't work, you know," she informed him shortly. "You're mad to think you can convince me to marry you."

"It's a risk," he replied, "but I have confidence in your good sense."

"I want the terms written down," she informed him, ignoring the compliment. "You wanted a business approach, and that's exactly how we'll handle this...this..."

"Courtship?" he offered.

She frowned and said, "Exercise in futility."

He chuckled. "Whatever. I suggest we meet to hash out the details over dinner tomorrow night. Phil is spending the evening with her grandparents. I know a wonderful little Italian place over on Riverside."

She was still frowning, as if trying to figure out how she'd been rooked. Finally she conceded. "Fine."

"Shall I pick you up?"

"I'll meet you there about seven."

"Seven it is."

She stared at him a moment longer, obviously confused about what he was doing and why. He kept his smile behind wraps until she gave up and simply retreated. She pointed at the contract, asking, "How are *you* going to explain that?"

He cocked his head, surprised that she would ask. "I'm the boss, Jolie," he said evenly. "I don't have to explain. How are you going to explain it?"

"Easy," she replied flippantly, wheeling toward the door. "I'll just tell my partners that the great Channing Hawkins has lost his everloving mind—and I took advantage of it."

He laughed and was still smiling long after she had gone, not that he expected an easy win. He was about to embark upon the campaign of his life—and it had nothing whatsoever to do with selling computers and everything to do with selling himself. True to form, he expected nothing but victory. Something told him, however, that the campaign itself would be a challenge unlike any other, and that when it was done, he'd find that he had relished every battle.

Satisfied, he wiped his palms on his thighs. Then he took

out a clean sheet of paper and began to jot down strategies by which a sensible man could get himself married.

Chan brought his beloved brick-red, extended-cab pickup truck—complete with running boards, bed liner, grill protector and heavy-duty bumpers—to a smooth stop curbside in front of the Fine Arts Center. A native Texan, he'd driven trucks since he'd been tall enough to slip behind the wheel of his father's three-quarter-ton farm hauler. He'd tried cars from time to time, but he'd always come back to the original Texas taxi, the cowboy limo. This particular jewel was less than five months old and absolutely everything a man could want, even a man more at home in chinos and polo shirts than jeans and brush-poppers. He cranked the air conditioner to maximum, opened the console and chose a favorite CD from the on-board collection, then slid it into the player. He saw no contradiction at all in a man who loved his truck but preferred his music rocked hard, heavily jazzed and/or deeply blue. By the time Phil shoved through the bank of glass doors fronting the building, wagging her violin case with one hand and music portfolio with the other, Channing was well on his way to happy and relaxed. Even the chore that lay ahead did not dim his bubbly sense of well-being.

He reached over and yanked open the passenger door as Phil approached the truck. She tossed her portfolio onto the back seat and carefully stashed the violin behind the front seat on the floor. She hauled herself up into her seat and reached for her seat belt, shouting, "Turn that down!"

Chan immediately lowered the volume of the sound system. "Sorry. Didn't realize I had it turned up so high."

Phil shoved the clip of her safety belt into the lock and slumped in censure. "You know, mostly it's *parents* who have to tell *kids* not to play their music so loud, *not* the other way around. Don't you *care* that you're ruining your hearing?"

"It wasn't *that* loud," he countered defensively.

"Anything over eighty decibels is a potential risk," she lectured, "and the older you get the greater the damage that can be done."

"Okay, already." He chuckled. "You make me sound like I've got one foot in the grave and the other on a banana peel."

"Don't you?" she retorted.

He didn't grace that with a reply, just started the truck rolling. "So how was your day?"

"Bor-r-ing."

Standard reply. "How was the music lesson?"

She brightened instantly. "Dr. Poe says I'm no prodigy, but with lots of practice I could be a competent violinist. I'm purely average in musical ability."

"Good for you," Chan said heartily, wondering how many other kids took such pleasure in being average at something. In Phil's case, she was either light years ahead of her contemporaries or, to hear her tell it, dead last. Average was something to aspire to in Phil's philosophy.

With endearingly typical-kid priorities, she abruptly wanted to know if they could eat at her favorite fast-food restaurant.

"Sure, why not?" he heard himself say, knowing that it was because of what was coming. He let several seconds pass, then cautiously announced, "I have something to tell you." He'd chosen his verbs carefully, wanting to let her know that he was mindful of her concern but unwilling to debate the issue.

She bounced in her seat absently. "Sure. What's up?"

He said it casually, letting her know it was a done deal. "I've asked Jolie Winters to marry me."

The horrified look that Phil turned on him could have scorched paint. "You *what?* Are you out of your mind? Why'd you go and do something stupid like that? You don't *like* her. She's a pasty-faced carrot-head! With freckles!"

"What's wrong with freckles?" he asked conversationally.

"I hate her!" Phil exclaimed. "I don't want her around. She's dumb. She's—"

"She hasn't said yes yet," he told her, ignoring the rest.

Phil folded her arms and slumped over them, glaring at him through narrowed eyes. "She doesn't want to marry you. She told me herself. You might as well forget it. She's too smart to think she could marry you for your money."

His mouth crooked into a smile. "Which is it, Phil, dumb or smart? Can't have it both ways, you know."

"I don't want you to get married again," she said in a small, plaintive voice.

"That's because you haven't thought it through honestly," he said, keeping his tone neutral. "I've been telling you for over two years now that we need a mom."

"Not that again!" Phil wailed.

"But you refuse to assess the situation unemotionally."

"I don't need a mother!"

"Sure you do," Channing retorted lightly.

"Okay," Phil snapped. "What for? Just tell me what for!"

"A girl needs a mom to talk to."

"About what? Sex? Periods? How to get boys? Number one, I know everything I need to about sex and don't *want* to know anything else. Number two, I probably know more about periods and all that stuff than your friendly neighborhood gynecologist. And number three, if I ever need to know what boys like, who better to tell me than you?"

"You always think you have everything figured out," he

said gently, "but despite all that brain power, you're just a nine-year-old kid. You need a mom. All kids need two parents."

"Do you know how many of the kids in my class have just one parent? Geez, Chan, don't you know that more than half of all marriages end in divorce?"

"Then I've got my half out of the way," he said brightly. "This one of my two will take, trust me."

"Don't I have anything to say about it?" she demanded. "It's my life, too, you know!"

"Sorry, kid. Parents rule."

"That's not funny!"

"You hear anybody laughing?"

"It's not fair," she sulked. "I won't let you do this."

"And just how do you figure to stop me?" he asked softly.

She hunched a shoulder sullenly and turned away from him. He knew what she was afraid of, not just of sharing him but of rejection. She couldn't understand that Jolie wasn't Amanda. No doubt Phil figured that he was sacrificing himself on her behalf, and he knew that he ought to punch a hole in that notion right off the bat, but how do you tell a nine-year-old of any IQ that you've lately developed a wholly natural but rather embarrassing hankering for a certain redhead's company under the sheets?

"Listen, kiddo," he began uncertainly, "this isn't really for you any more than it is for me. I like being married, and Jolie's just what I've been looking for. I know it'll be different, sharing our lives and space with someone else, but it's all going to work out for the best, trust me."

Phil said nothing, nor did she turn her face from the window. Channing let it go, figuring that only time would prove to her that he was doing the best thing for both of them.

She was a smart kid. Heck, she was a genius! She'd figure it all out soon enough.

"So what do you want for dinner?" he asked to utter silence. "I'm going for the big combo with that banana milk shake," he went on undeterred. "Onion rings, maybe, instead of fries. Guess you'll be wanting salad and diet soda."

She turned a pained expression on him, not thawing yet, but considering it. "I'll have a greasy burger and fries coated an inch-thick with salt. And a side order of strychnine."

He chuckled, wondering for which one of them she meant the side order. Him, most likely. Well, she'd get over it. When she saw all that Jolie could bring to their household, she'd relax and enjoy. Then she would be glad he'd given her a chance at normalcy, at family and all that came with it. He was so smugly sure of himself that he forgot the first rule of good planning: Never take anything for granted.

Jolie fought down the urge to glance at her reflection in the window of the restaurant as she charged reluctantly up the slanting walk. The summer heat was broiling her alive, even though the evening cool-down had started. She refused to think that the long, many-layered, gauze broomstick skirt she'd chosen to wear with mules and a fringed crocheted vest over a simple T-shirt might have anything to do with her discomfort. Dessie had told her flatly that she looked like a bag lady in the making, but Jolie had not been able to convince herself that wearing a miniskirt was the thing to do. Too much had been said about her legs for her comfort. Wearing a short skirt and putting them on display would signal that she actually believed his blather and desired more of his unbelievable compliments. So the broomstick skirt—and heat rash—it was.

The hostess of the sleepy little restaurant greeted her with a knowing smile. "Are you meeting Chan?"

"Ah, yes, as a matter of fact, I am."

"Just follow me."

They walked past a small bar crammed with quiet, relaxed people and wound through a dining room where every table was filled. Glasses clinked and voices murmured, but the noise level was surprisingly low for such a capacity crowd, especially considering the resonant qualities of the bare, cracked cement floor and flat, unadorned stucco ceiling. The atmosphere was one of supreme leisure. The decor was rough and unimaginative, but no one seemed to care.

The young, petite, college-age hostess led her into a section of the dining room screened off by lattice thinly covered with plastic grapevine. It was darker here and sparsely populated, with only two couples at widely spaced booths and Channing Hawkins at another. His head was bent over a file folder, pen in one hand, wineglass in the other. He looked up as they walked over and beamed a high-wattage smile at her. Candle flame reflected off the lenses of his glasses. Springing to his feet, he kissed the cheek belonging, not to Jolie but the hostess.

"Thanks, sugar. Did she put up much of a fight?"

The hostess giggled, betraying her youth, and spun away with the sweep of a ponytail. "As if. I'll send Juno right over."

"Tell him to bring another glass of Lambrusco," he called before turning his gaze on Jolie. "You really have to try this stuff. It's great."

"I usually prefer Chianti," she muttered stubbornly, sliding into the booth.

"Yeah? Well, when it comes to wine, I'm a soda-pop drinker. I'll take the Lambrusco and you can order a Chianti, if you want."

But when the wine appeared, she sipped and found it very much to her liking, drat him. While she pretended not to care about her wine, the waiter, Juno, who also sported a ponytail, rattled off the specials. Channing quickly decided on the chicken parmigiana stuffed with mushrooms and shrimp, vermicelli and an artichoke salad. Jolie mulled over pepper steak and calamari, then settled for pork diavollo and spaghetti with a traditional Caesar salad. Hot, fragrant, steaming bread drenched in olive oil and spices appeared. Jolie's stomach rumbled hungrily. She'd been too nervous to do much with her lunch, and now it was catching up with her. Channing broke off a generous hunk of bread, dumped it on a plate and shoved it over to her. He stuck a smaller piece in his mouth. Then, without the barest preliminaries, he got right down to business.

"I took the liberty of drawing up a document that I think is eminently fair to both of us. Want to take a glance?"

She didn't bother to comment about this being a weird way to start a so-called courtship, but then again, this was a weird courtship if ever there was one. Actually, she reminded herself, it was no courtship at all. It was a trade-off, nothing more, an exercise in futility, just as she'd told him. She'd barely scratched the surface of his "contract" when she found serious grounds for objection.

"Oh, no. I am *not* moving in with you."

"Hey, it's a big house. What better way to get a feel for—"

"No." She leaned forward and said again, just in case he didn't hear it the first time, "No."

He sighed, reached across the paper and struck through the clause with his pen. "Okay, okay. I'll settle for an occasional overnighter, a weekend here and there."

She fought down the sense of victory and narrowed her eyes at him, reminding herself what a tough negotiator he was reputed to be, though in all honesty she'd seen little of that. "Let's get this straight right off. Under no circumstances will I sleep with you."

"Not even after we're married?" he asked cutely.

"We won't *be* married."

"Because I really think Phil needs siblings," he went on calmly. "I'd like one more, I really would, maybe two."

Heat rushed up Jolie's throat from her belly. Children. He wanted more children. For some reason, panic expanded her chest. She shook her head. "I—I've never seen myself as a mother."

"Really?" He cocked his head, studying her blatantly. "I very much see you as a mother."

"That's because you *want* to see me that way," she snapped dismissively, finding it difficult to look at him. "I'm not good with babies. Ask Dessie, my partner. She has a little girl, Mona, and—"

"She brings her to the office," he interrupted. "Yes, you mentioned that. It's a funny thing, though. Before I adopted Phil, those first three years of her life when she was the very center of Donnelly's universe, I couldn't see myself in his shoes. I was married then, and Amanda really didn't want children. We agreed on that. Then Don got sick, and he asked me to take Phil, and I fought it at first, but then this feeling started building in me, like maybe I really could and should be a father." He drew a design on the butcher paper covering the table top with his pen. "The decision to take Phil cost me my marriage, you know, but I'll tell you something, I'd do it all over again. Phil has brought more to my life than Amanda ever could have, but that's because Amanda was the wrong woman for me. I don't have any doubt about that. You, on the other hand, are another matter. I'm not wrong about you, Jolie. I'm not. You're the right one, I know it."

"But what about love?" she heard herself ask, and was instantly appalled.

"Well, there's love and then there's love," he said carefully, still doodling on the table paper. "I want a wiser, saner kind of love this time, one that develops gradually with mutual respect and certain upfront guarantees instead of this explosion of unreasonable urges and uncontrollable lusts. I won't try to tell you that I love you now. That would be ludicrous. But I honestly think that will come."

Unreasonable urges and uncontrollable lusts. Jolie felt a sharp pain beneath her ribs. He wanted a woman who would not inspire in him unreasonable urges and uncontrollable lusts. And *she* was that woman. She should be glad. This whole thing was so absurd that she should really be glad. Instead she felt oddly wounded and perilously close to tears. Angry at herself, she snatched up the proposal he'd drawn up and began to read it again. After a moment, she reached over and snatched the pen out of his hand, marking out and rewriting.

She rather enjoyed the actual negotiation, and the diavollo was spectacular, hot as firecrackers, just the way she liked it. When they were done, the parameters were firmly set. Sex was out. Reasonable and respectful displays of affection were permissible, both in public and private. She would not move in with him. She would spend several evenings a week with him and/or Phil and occasionally stay the night when the circumstances dictated. Neither of them would see anyone else during the contracted period. They would take turns choosing recreational activities. Introductions to family would be delayed until a final decision was made about their future prospects. Whether or not to introduce each other to friends would be made on a case by case basis, depending on the situation.

They wrangled longest over who would pay for what,

with Chan contending that he should pay all expenses because the concept had originated with him, and Jolie contending that she preferred to pay her own way. They finally hashed out a reasonable plan. In fact, the whole thing was patently reasonable and terribly, terribly impersonal, so much so that Jolie was flatly depressed by the time they finished their cappuccino and ices. Oddly enough, the easiest items had concerned Phil. Chan had warned Jolie that she was in for a bumpy ride as far as Phil was concerned, but agreed that she should deal with it in her own way without undue interference from him. She figured Phil would be no problem because she intended to tell the girl the whole deal. Phil had nothing to worry about from her, nothing at all.

When he walked her to her car later, she was surprised to find how many hours had elapsed. It was still hot and sticky outside, but the night had a velvet feel about it that literally caressed the skin. Channing's hand rested lightly in the small of her back as they walked, side by side, bobbing discordantly, across the nearly empty parking lot.

"Well, good night," she said, after unlocking her door.

He brushed a kiss across her mouth. "Good night."

She frowned as he turned and walked away, sliding his hands into his pockets and whistling softly. She got into the car, then watched him climb into an expensively customized truck. Only then did she admit to herself that she was feeling a crushing disappointment.

Chapter Five

The door opened before Jolie even reached it. Casting a furtive look over one shoulder, Phil stepped outside and closed the door behind her.

"You lied to me!"

"I did not."

"You said you weren't interested in romance."

"I'm not."

"Then why are you marrying Chan?"

"I'm not!"

"Then what are you doing here?"

Jolie brought her hands to her waist and reluctantly admitted, "I agreed contractually to give Chan ninety days to try to change my mind about marrying him."

Phil's eyes went as wide as the lenses of her glasses, and she threw up her arms. "What kind of an idiot lets herself get *contracted* for something like that?"

Jolie folded her arms and said, "The kind with a business and partnership to protect."

Phil's eyes abruptly narrowed. "Oh, come on. Chan would never threaten—"

"Oh, wouldn't he? Not outright, perhaps, but he sure made me a sweetheart deal when I agreed to his demands. Honestly, what would you have done, Phil? My partners were depending on me, and one of them has a baby to support all by herself."

Phil shook her head, long hair rippling. "This just doesn't make any sense. Chan's not the sort to throw his weight around." The look she fixed on Jolie was surprisingly desperate. "What are we going to do?"

"Nothing," Jolie said, placing a comforting hand on the girl's shoulder. "I'm going to give Channing his ninety days, then we'll all go our separate ways."

Phil rolled her eyes. "You really are stupid, aren't you? Chan plays for keeps. He always has a plan. You can't underestimate him."

"I don't. He's the one who has underestimated me," Jolie insisted, "and I don't appreciate being called stupid. I won't stand for that kind of abuse, Phil. I really won't."

Phil threw up her hands. "Why won't you listen to me? You're not as immune to his schemes and plans as you think you are." Her eyes narrowed to elongated slits. "Or are you playing us both? Maybe you have your own plan working here. Maybe you're just pretending."

Jolie sighed. "Trust me, Phil. I'm not that Machiavellian. I really don't want to marry anyone, especially not Channing Hawkins."

The child glared at her suspiciously. "Why not? It's me, isn't it? You don't want kids, but especially not one like me."

"That's not true," Jolie assured her, shaken. "I just don't want to be married. There's no reason the two of us can't be friends, though."

"Why would I want to be your friend?" Phil asked snidely. "You're just a dumb old maid trying to get her claws into a good thing. You don't really like me. You're just after—"

"That's enough," Jolie commanded, a little surprised when Phil actually complied, clamping her mouth shut mulishly. Suddenly the girl whirled around and shoved her way into the house, hair flying in a blond arc. Jolie stood in the opened doorway for a moment, listening to the sound of Phil pounding her way up the stairs to her left and feeling pretty battered herself. The interior of the house was cool and inviting. Slowly, Jolie ventured inside and pulled the door closed behind her. The feeling of otherworldliness that she had felt before once more enveloped her. She took a good look around her, wondering where Chan was and how she ought to proceed. Finally she ventured farther into the entry hall and called out his name.

He appeared almost instantly from the kitchen, wiping his hands dry on a dish towel. A smile split his face. "Hey! I didn't hear the bell."

Jolie made a quick assessment and decided that no purpose would be served in telling him about her encounter with his daughter. "Phil let me in," she said truthfully, just that.

He craned his neck to inspect all the nooks and crannies behind her, asking, "Where is she?"

"Uh, she went upstairs."

"Back to the computer, no doubt," he supplied. He jerked his head toward the kitchen. "Come on in. I'm just cleaning up after supper. Want some dessert?"

"No, thanks."

"How about a drink then?"

"I suppose."

She remained doggedly unenthusiastic as he led her into

the kitchen, parked her on a bar stool and poured her a glass of white wine without asking her preference. She sipped, lifted an eyebrow in obvious appreciation and sipped again. Chan turned back to his chores and quickly finished wiping down the countertops.

"You're awfully neat." She hadn't meant to make it sound like an accusation, but she bit back an apology anyway.

"The product of an orderly mind, I suppose," he said with a taut smile.

She said nothing to that, just sipped her wine. He folded the dish towel and laid it aside. "I thought we'd watch a tape. I have a bunch we've never watched. Want to look them over?"

She slid off the stool with the same lack of enthusiasm as she'd climbed onto it. "If you like."

He led her into the family room, showed her where he'd stacked the videos and suggested that she look them over while he went upstairs to fetch Phil. After ten minutes he returned without his daughter, saying that she was busy on her computer. Jolie was sitting cross-legged on the floor, videos stacked in piles around her. He vaulted over the back of the couch and plopped down in its center.

"Find anything?"

She shrugged noncommittally. He had enough videos to stock a small store. "Depends. You up for action/adventure, tear-jerker, social commentary or subtitles?" She pointed from one pile to another as she detailed the choices, carefully omitting the romances as an option.

He spread his hands. "Makes no never mind to me."

She let him know with a look that this reply was not appreciated.

Instantly repentant, he said, "Okay, let's try this. What's your favorite movie of all time?"

"That's easy," she said, *"Singin' in the Rain."*

He got up and went to the built-in cabinet around the television, opening doors to reveal row upon row of videos. Make that a large store, she thought wryly. "I don't have that one, but I do have a few other old musicals, mostly Shirley Temple, I'm afraid."

She wrinkled her nose, then gave in to the impulse to turn his question on him. "So what's your favorite movie of all time?"

"The Maltese Falcon," he replied immediately.

Surprised, she barked a doubtful laugh, and he turned a smile over one shoulder.

"What?"

"It's just, I figured you for a special effects man."

"Well, that's always interesting, of course, but special effects are just that. They don't exactly make a movie, you know. To me, the only real marriage of the two is animation. I love animation." He waved at a whole row of animated movies.

"Really?" She got up off the floor and joined him in front of the cabinet, reading the titles aloud. She plucked one from the shelf. "Oh, I *love* this."

"Yeah?" He took down another. "Ever seen this one?"

She turned it over in her hand. "No. Is this new?"

"Came out last year."

"Well, I haven't seen an animated movie in a long time. I mean, they're for kids."

"I know a great many adults who would argue that point," he said, "myself included. In fact, some animated movies are suitable for adults only, and very broad-minded adults at that."

"Is this one of those?" she asked, quickly handing the video back to him.

He chuckled. "Nope. This one's strictly G-rated."

Relieved, she turned away, saying off-handedly, "Oh. Might as well take a look then."

He slid the video into the machine and waved her down onto the couch, taking a place beside her. Aiming the remote, he started the player and settled back. He lifted his arm, as if intending to loop it about her shoulders, and she automatically stiffened. At the last moment, he derailed the action. Jolie frowned, not liking that her relief was so heavily tinged with disappointment. She fixed her attention on the film, and was soon engrossed, finding the characters and story quite charming.

Chan watched her watching the film, glad that she had chosen something with which he was so very familiar. He wasn't surprised that she seemed to be enjoying the film, but he was pleased. He had known instinctively that they would have a great deal in common. Something about Jolie felt right to him, as if she belonged. He couldn't understand why she didn't feel it or why she wouldn't admit it if she did. But then, women were an enigma. Better men than him had tried and failed to understand the female viewpoint, which was precisely why he knew that Phil had to have a mother.

It was all so perfectly logical that he couldn't for the life of him figure out why Phil and Jolie couldn't see the beauty of his plan. It *had* to be a female thing, but it wasn't going to defeat him. This was right. He was right. He knew it with the same instinctive confidence that had brought him together with Donnelly Phillips and had helped the business to grow tenfold since Donnelly's death.

He knew also that he probably should have insisted that Phil come down and join them. She and Jolie needed to get to know each other, after all, and he didn't fool himself that it would be easy. Phil was never really approachable, and she already had erected barriers against Jolie, but Channing was convinced that Jolie could and would eventually overcome them. All the more reason to have made Phil come down. On the other hand, he rationalized, Jolie needed some one-on-one time with him, too, time to realize that he was not a nutcase looking for someone upon whom to dump his domestic problems, but rather a man who intended to take into his personal life the same intuitive logic that had served him so well in business. It would be safer, though, if Phil were there. He was less likely to let his physical interest overwhelm his good sense that way, but then, he was an adult. He would manage.

Crossing his legs, he grabbed his ankle and held on, quelling the urge to wrap his arm around Jolie and pull her close. The impulse to do so remained strong, seeming as natural as breathing. Taking her to bed would be like that, natural, uninhibited, free—if she would just make up her mind to let it happen. Not that he intended to press it. For one thing, he was a man of his word. For another, he judged that it was best to take things slowly with her. Success with Jolie would be built one small step at a time. Rushing her would merely harden her resolve.

He knew that she was purposefully dampening her responses, but he wasn't particularly worried about it. She couldn't keep that up indefinitely. Masking interest required a lot of energy. She certainly wasn't succeeding with the video.

She laughed at a gooney bird attempting to correct his inability to fly with tiny rockets strapped to his ankles, and her whole face lit softly from within. He wanted to kiss every one of those freckles, watch the light in her bronze-brown eyes slowly build to a flame hot enough to consume them both. But he was a patient man. He could wait—and relish the reality all the more for it.

His senses were so finely tuned, so enlivened, by the woman next to him, that he was instantly aware of his daughter as she crept to the door of the family room. He waited expectantly for her to join them and, when she did not, casually shifted his position in order to view the door. A flash of ash-blond hair as she yanked back out of sight alerted him that her purpose was not to join them but to spy upon them. Smiling grimly to himself, he eased to one side and slumped into the corner of the long sofa. Phil was soon convinced that nothing of interest was to be seen and slipped away. Let them both think that his plan was inept and unfocused. By the time they realized otherwise, he'd have made a family of the three of them. He was absolutely sure of it. Patience was the key. And he was a man known for his patience. He wouldn't let that long-cultivated attribute desert him now, despite the temptation sitting next to him. He would keep his hands to himself, and in the end, he would reap the rewards of his restraint. He shoved his hands into his pants pockets and contemplated the future—and a time when indulgence would replace patience.

Jolie thoroughly enjoyed the video, so much so that afterward she found herself quickly engaged in a spirited conversation about the characters, the story line and the production values. Only when Channing poked her in the ribs with a long, blunt forefinger and laughingly called her a secret fairy-tale junkie did she realize what she was doing. Taking herself in hand, she sternly reminded herself that she could not, under any circumstances, warm up to Channing Hawkins. He would totally misread any relaxation on her part and be quick to take advantage.

She cleared her throat and popped up from the couch. "I should be going. I, er, have things to do."

"You sure? I thought we might have that dessert now. I have a frozen pie in the—"

She cut him off with a shake of her head. "No, thanks. I'm not hungry. You go ahead. I'll just let myself out." She moved sideways toward the door, but he was on his feet and already moving toward her.

"Don't be silly. If you really have to go, I'll walk you out."

"I really have to go," she lied uneasily, wondering why she felt the need to do so. "You know how it is. A thousand things to do. Work tomorrow."

He didn't reply to that, just lifted a hand and invited her to precede him into the hallway. She did so quickly. He fell into step beside her two long strides later.

"The weatherman's predicting a hot, dry weekend with moderate winds," he said conversationally.

"Oh? That's nice."

"Good weekend for the lake. Thought you might join us."

"I, ah—"

"You're not bailing on me, are you?" he interrupted conversationally. "We have a verbal contract with the intents on paper, you know."

As if she needed reminding! "I'm not bailing on you," she retorted sharply.

"Well, you'll come early then," he said lightly, making it a marginal question, "and plan to stay overnight?"

She started to tell him that she had other plans, but then she reconsidered. Better to get it out of the way, to let him see that he wasn't going to make any headway with her. Still, she was loath to merely capitulate. "We'll see," she stated flatly.

"Does that mean you're not coming?" he asked, stopping in front of the door.

"I'll be here Saturday," she said tensely. "We'll see about spending the night."

He opened his mouth as if to protest, but then he closed it again sheepishly. After a moment he said, "I hope you enjoyed the evening as much as I did."

She didn't want to lie to him or seem unnecessarily rude, so she settled for a wan smile and an abrupt nod and said, "I really have to go."

"Thanks for coming." He reached for the doorknob, but his hand merely covered it. She looked up expectantly and gave him a perfect opportunity to kiss her, which he did quickly on the mouth, grinning down at her afterward with all the pride in accomplishment of a one-year-old taking his first steps. Her first impulse was to tell him to do the thing properly or not at all, but then she realized what she'd be opening herself up to and scowled. He chuckled, the wretch, and opened the door, saying cheerfully, "See you Saturday."

She mumbled a good-night and slipped past him, head down. She was still mumbling about the stupidity of what she'd almost done and said as she walked across the drive to her car. A figure suddenly popped up from behind the fender. She yelped before she recognized Phil.

"Shh! I don't want him to know I'm talking to you."

Jolie leaned a hip against the car and frowned at the girl. "You scared me."

"We have to change his mind," she said, waving away Jolie's fright as inconsequential. "He's just doing this because he thinks I need a mother."

"He's probably right about that—" Jolie began.

"He is not!"

"—just not me," she finished firmly.

"That's what we have to make him believe," Phil announced. "He doesn't want you for himself. I was watching, and he didn't touch you, didn't even try to hold your hand. So what we've got to do is convince him that you'd be a lousy mother."

"Now wait a minute," Jolie said, miffed that Phil was so easily convinced of her lack of appeal to a man such as Channing, not to mention her ability to rear a child. "I could be a good—or, at least, an okay—mother."

"That's not the point," Phil insisted, stamping a foot impatiently. "I'm talking about the quickest way to get this stupid idea about marrying you out of Chan's head. If we convince him that you'd make a lousy mother, he'll drop you. Don't you see?"

Jolie did see, and it was the perfect solution. So why did it make her stomach sour? She pushed away the feeling. "How would you suggest we go about that?"

Phil shrugged entirely too nonchalantly. "Just let him see how much you dislike me."

"But I don't dislike you, Phil."

Phil snorted. "I'm not an idiot!"

"True. But you are wrong. I don't dislike you at all. I meant it when I said that we could be friends."

Phil stared at her, and for a long moment Jolie saw the hunger behind the belligerence, but then Phil shook her head stubbornly. "We don't need you," she said firmly. "I don't need you, no matter what Chan thinks." With that she turned and fled, leaving Jolie completely convinced that she did, indeed, need someone, despite her protests. For the first time, Jolie understood what had driven Chan to take these extraordinary steps. Disturbed, Jolie got into her car and drove away, telling herself that it wasn't her problem—and wondering why she couldn't quite believe it.

She fought with herself about it, waffling back and forth right up to the moment Saturday morning when she yanked the overnight bag from beneath the bed and began throwing things into it. All the while she told herself, aloud and in no uncertain terms, what a glutton for punishment she was, what a fool, what a sentimental weakling. Without planning or forethought she threw a pair of jeans, a T-shirt, a sundress, a nightie and a few underthings into the bag, tossed in a variety of hair ribbons and clips, a lipstick and a comb and a toothbrush. Then she donned a simple, one-piece, black halter-top bathing suit with high-cut legs, black jogging shorts and a white crocheted top. White sandals and a white plastic bow on a clip for her hair completed the ensemble. Stuffing her purse with a paperback novel, sunshades and a tube of sun block, she grabbed the overnight bag and hauled the lot out of her small apartment and down the stairs to her car.

Almost twenty minutes later she pulled up in front of the fairy-tale mansion of Channing Hawkins and got out. After several long moments, he opened the door himself.

"Hi." Spotting her overnight bag, he literally beamed at her and hastened to take it from her, though it was light enough. Inside the foyer, he stepped back and swept her from head to toe with an appreciative gaze. "You look great. Glad you wore your suit. I want to get out on the lake today. Phil is already down at the dock, pouting about it."

"She doesn't like the water?"

"She doesn't like anything athletic," he said easily. "Let me show you your room, then we'll go down and join her." He started up the stairs on the right. Wide and deep, the steps spiraled up the turret, which was lit by tall, multipaned, leaded-glass windows and a heavy brass fixture suspended from the coned ceiling by a thick chain. "We have six bedrooms," he was saying, "three on this side, three on Phil's, with an exercise room, playroom and music room between."

"Music room?" she repeated, curious despite herself.

"Sure. I'll show you around." He moved to the end of the long, wide hall and threw open the last door on the right, revealing a huge bedroom furnished with a couch and chair in bamboo, an enormous bed with a headboard constructed of what looked like elephant tusks, a desk, chest of drawers, armoire and a big, comfy-looking rocker. The lamps were made of colorfully woven baskets and painted clay pots. Teak floors, cushions and the bed itself were covered with what appeared to be the hides of exotic animals: zebra, tiger, water buffalo and others she didn't recognize.

"These aren't real, are they?" she asked anxiously, indicating the hides.

"Very expensive fakes," he answered. "Even the tusks. The masks and shields are all authentic, though." He stepped inside and indicated the walls, which were covered with African artifacts, including a few lethal-looking spears, and several large, framed photographs. "I brought them all back from safari in Africa, including the photos, which were the only things I shot or intended to."

Jolie looked around her in awe, spellbound by the contents of the room, including the plants tucked into the corners and hanging in front of the windows, big, leafy ferns and even one palm tree. One wall was mirrored, including the door, which stood open on a large bath opulently furnished with ivory-white and dark-brown fixtures, including a sunken tub at least six feet wide. The room was so clean that a surgeon could have operated in there. The balcony behind the windows looked out over the lake.

"This is incredible," she murmured.

"Thanks," he said. "I like it. Remind me to show you the rest of my pictures from Africa sometime. In fact, remind me to show you Africa."

She rolled her eyes at that, but inside she felt a spurt of

sheer covetousness. She would *so* like to see Africa, especially after experiencing that room. Chuckling, he led her back into the hallway and to the next door. This room, too, was large but furnished in tame French provincial, all ivory and delicate peach with the exception of an enormous antique tapestry that completely covered one wall. "Fifteenth century," he informed her, dropping her overnight bag on the embroidered silk bedspread. "Picked it up in France." He walked over to one of a pair of doors and thrust it open, revealing a private bath.

They wandered from room to room, each revealing treasures brought from around the world. One room was Chinese, all black lacquer and deep reds, hand-painted silks and delicate porcelains. Another was Spanish, with smooth whitewashed walls and sturdy, studded furniture, ornate wrought iron and heavy velvets. An authentic matador's costume had been pinned to one wall, along with the ears and tail of a bull. Its neighbor had been furnished with materials brought from Peru, a framed photo of Chan and Phil and a Peruvian family in native costume attesting to the fact that it had been decorated as a monument to an unforgettable experience.

The final room was Phil's. A typical little girl's canopied bed with a pink ruffled spread took center stage in front of a similarly draped window, but the only toys in sight were a number of dolls dressed in the native costumes of all the countries they had visited and an Erector Set on a table. Bookshelves lined the walls, filled with volumes on astronomy, computer science, mechanics, mathematics, paleontology and so on. A computer with a twenty-one-inch monitor, a printer and a plotter and more than enough other equipment to open a small business filled one corner and spilled over into the room, which was kid-messy and scattered with discarded bits of clothing and paper. Jolie found herself wanting to linger there and explore the nooks and crannies, but the knowledge that Phil would not welcome this invasion of her privacy sent her out the door again.

The exercise room turned out to be as well equipped as any gym. The playroom included a blackboard, drawing tables and art supplies and showed little evidence of having been used. The music room contained a dance floor, jukebox, enough stereo equipment to open a club, and an impressive collection of CDs, as well as a number of comfortable chairs and a lone music stand next to an open violin case.

"Whose violin?" she asked.

"Phil's," he said, adding proudly, "she's happily average at best."

Jolie lifted both brows thoughtfully. "I guess it's hard to be average when you're as smart as she is."

"I think it's hard to be average, period," he said wisely, "but it's especially difficult for her. And speaking of Phil, I think we'd better be getting down to the water."

They hurried downstairs and through the first floor to the terrace, then across the lawn and down to the dock. A chest-type cooler, table, umbrella and chairs had been set up on the planking. A variety of watercraft was tied to the pier. Phil sat with her bare feet drawn up in her chair, a hardback book balanced on her knees. She wore her regular uniform of shorts and oversize T-shirt, but Jolie noted the string of a bathing suit tied behind her neck. The bill of a baseball cap shaded her face.

"Jolie's here," Chan announced as they drew near. Phil said nothing, just turned the page in her book. Chan walked to the water's edge and stooped to untie a line looped about a small cleat, saying, "Why don't you two keep each other company while I test the wind? Cold drinks in the chest, Jolie. Help yourself."

"Thanks. I will." She pulled out a chair and sat down close to the cooler. Lifting the lid, she poked around until she found an ice-cold bottle of root beer. It foamed when she twisted off the cap, and she captured the yummy stuff in her mouth. She'd fished her shades out of her purse earlier and hung them on the neck of her top by the earpiece. Now she plucked them free and slid them onto her face. By the time she'd consumed half her soda, Chan had peeled off his shirt, donned a life jacket and was on the water, paddling out astride what looked like a thick red surfboard, until he fitted a pole into a slot and raised a bright yellow sail. When he stood on the board, displaying an unexpectedly generous expanse of sun-bronzed skin, Jolie quickly turned her attention to the girl.

"What're you reading?" she asked idly, unsurprised when Phil failed to answer. Jolie sat forward and placed her drink on the table, forearms folded in front of it. "You can ignore me, Phil, but I won't go away, not until I'm good and ready."

The girl glared at her over the top of her book. "What do you care what I'm reading?"

"Ever heard of polite conversation?" Jolie asked. "The key word there is *polite.*"

"I don't want you here."

Jolie sighed inwardly, but she knew somehow that this wasn't personal. "We've established that, and also that I'm not going to go away until I've fulfilled my contract with Chan," she said casually. "What's he doing, anyway?"

"It's called windsurfing," Phil answered in a rude tone.

"Looks like fun."

"Huh. Looks boring to me. I'd rather read."

"Gosh, he's good, isn't he?"

"Good at risking his life," Phil muttered.

"Doesn't look all that dangerous to me," Jolie said lightly.

Phil closed her book and set it aside. "Do you have any idea how deep that water is?"

"No, but I'd bet he's a strong swimmer."

Phil made a face, as if to say that swimming was overrated. "People drown all the time," she pointed out, "and lots of them are strong swimmers."

"People die all sorts of ways, Phil, a great many of them from health problems due to inactivity. You should be glad that Chan's athletic and fit."

Phil looked away, but not before Jolie caught the shadow of genuine concern in her eyes. She was coming to understand that this kid was a bundle of worries, and most of them seemed to have to do with the fear of abandonment. Jolie remembered the cramps in her stomach that she used to get whenever her mother or father were late for a visit, which was most of the time, and suddenly her heart went out to the girl. "Chan showed me around upstairs," she said impulsively. "The two of you have obviously been all over the world together. Were you ever frightened then?"

Phil's face lit with remembered adventures, but she quickly tamped down her enthusiasm, shrugging sullenly. "Sometimes. Not often. Once in Africa we almost got trampled by an elephant. Chan clicked a picture and it just went nuts. The guide told us later that it had just given birth. They're very protective of their young, you know."

Jolie nodded, keeping her smile out of sight. "They're matriarchal, aren't they, traveling in family groups?"

"That's right, and they're very emotional. I read about this elephant in India recently that grieved to death after her companion died. They say she shed real tears."

"How sad."

Phil went on talking on the subject for several minutes,

her young face grave as she spilled out fact after fact. Jolie had never particularly wondered about the actual thickness of an elephant's skin, but she found Phil's interest most fascinating. Chan paddled back into the dock, and Phil didn't even notice, so intent was she on imparting every bit of knowledge that she'd learned on the subject of elephants.

"Telling her about the one that nearly got us in Africa?" Chan asked, picking up a towel from the chair directly opposite Jolie and mopping his face with it. Jolie knew the exact moment when Phil realized how long and easily she'd been talking. She clammed up instantly.

"How's the water?" Jolie asked, deftly changing the subject.

"Wonderful, and the wind is perfect. Do you windsurf?"

"Never have, nope."

"Want to try?"

Jolie opened her mouth to admit that she would, then slid a glance at Phil. "Yeah, sure, unless Phil wants to first."

Channing easily read her intent. He went on casually toweling off. "How about it, Phil? Want to go out with me?"

Phil frowned. "I don't—"

"Or shall I take Jolie?" Channing interrupted calmly.

"—mind if I do," Phil finished, her chin jutting out.

Channing grinned at Jolie. "If you get bored—"

"You could always just leave," Phil interrupted sharply.

Channing frowned at her and said, "You need a vest and water socks, not to mention an attitude adjustment."

Phil slashed a narrow gaze at Jolie, letting her know that she was aware of the manipulation and had agreed to this for her own reasons. Yanking off her glasses, she dropped them onto the table and muttered a guttural apology.

"No problem," Jolie said, just as if the apology had actually been meant for her. Chan winked and led his daughter to the end of the pier. Phil lifted her chin and marched off as if to the guillotine. Jolie picked up Phil's book and read the title on the spine. "Managing Your Manager." She chortled as the implications made themselves clear. Like father, like daughter. Always take the business approach. She couldn't help wondering which one of them would come out on top.

Chapter Six

Jolie eventually realized that Phil was keeping her father out on the water as long as she possibly could. Well over an hour passed before father and daughter returned to the pier. Phil might have been any happy little girl in that moment, her small face beaming with the obvious success of her venture.

"That was fun!"

"It certainly was," Channing agreed.

"Let's go back out," she pleaded.

"Time you tried it on your own," Chan replied. "You can do it."

She shook her head. "Not without my glasses, I can't."

"Well, you can't take a chance on losing them, and you wouldn't let me buy you one of those sports straps," Chan pointed out.

Phil made a face. "Okay, okay, so I was a goober. Can't you take me back out for now?"

"Let me rest for a bit, will you?" Chan said, chuckling.

"We can rig a safety strap," Jolie spoke up. "All we need is some ribbon or string."

"How about a shoestring?" Chan suggested.

"If it's long enough."

He quickly stripped one out of Phil's own athletic shoe and handed it to Jolie. "Now the way you do this," she said, making a loop and tying the ends to it, "is like so." She slid the ends back and forth, demonstrating how it could be made to fit. Phil quickly caught on to the concept. Practically snatching the string out of Jolie's hands, she quickly looped the sides around the ear pieces of her glasses, put them on, then adjusted the string for a snug fit.

"Watch this!" she exclaimed, running for the end of the pier.

"After you thank Jolie," Chan said firmly.

Phil grumbled a thank you, then called out, "Watch me, Chan," as she mounted the surfer.

"I'm watching."

"Promise!"

"I won't take my eyes off you," he vowed. "Just don't go out too far."

He stood next to the table, eyes shaded with his hands and watched as Phil paddled out, set the sail and got up onto the board. "Thanks," he said without so much as glancing at Jolie.

"I didn't do anything really."

"We both know better." He chanced a quick look. "You got her out on the water. Now just look at her. Somehow, you understand her."

"She's afraid of losing you," Jolie said quietly.

"It's more than that," Chan replied, waving to Phil to prove that he was watching her every move. "She remembers more than she should. You wouldn't think a three-year-old could, but then she wasn't your average three-year-old."

"Donnelly's death, you mean."

"And Amanda's rejection," he said bitterly. "My ex-wife."

Jolie caught her breath. He had said that adopting Phil had cost him his marriage, but she hadn't understood exactly what he'd meant. "Are you telling me that Amanda left you because you adopted Phil?"

He dropped a frank glance on her. "Exactly."

"And Phil knows that?"

"It would have been hard not to with Amanda shrieking that she wouldn't raise 'that freak' for love or money."

Jolie's stomach dropped, leaving a hollow, empty feeling inside her. For a moment, she could barely breathe.

"Look, Chan!" Phil called, her voice sounding small and childish.

He cupped his hands around his mouth. "You're doing great!"

Jolie couldn't see for the shadows of pain clouding her own eyes. A freak. Amanda had called—had considered—Phil a freak. How many other times must the girl have heard that word? No wonder she didn't believe anyone would really like her but Channing. What weapons of pain words could be. How many times had her own mother lamented "those spots," as she'd called Jolie's freckles, and unwittingly wounded her daughter in the process? How much worse to hear yourself called a freak, especially after just having lost your father to illness? What young child could handle such viciousness? Suddenly Phil's animosity made terrible sense.

"I hope you told Amanda who the real freak was," Jolie said through stiff lips.

Chan smiled coldly. "Let's just say I helped Amanda pack."

Jolie felt a fierce sense of gratification at that. "Good."

He chuckled. "And you say you have no mothering instincts."

"I didn't say that," she retorted.

"You implied it."

And so she had. Consequently, she didn't bother denying it. Instead she said, "Have you considered that Phil and I might do better as friends than parent and child?"

He pulled a chair around and sat down in it, waving at Phil to let her know he was still watching. "A friend would be a poor second to a mother," he said. "Besides, Phil isn't the only one with something to gain from having you as her mother." He reached across the table and covered her hand with his, never taking his gaze from his daughter "I really do want you for my wife, you know," he said softly.

Heat poured through Jolie as his fingers curled around hers. Once more, she was having difficulty catching her breath. A longing as surprising as it was fierce seized her, so that she found herself clutching his hand. Several long moments passed before her head cleared enough for reason to reassert itself. Of course he would say that. He had to say that. He would do or say anything for his daughter. She quickly disengaged from his touch, but not before Phil had seen them holding hands on top of the table.

Channing chuckled as the girl quickly dropped sail and paddled back to shore. "Okay, your turn," he declared, hopping up from his chair and looking down at her.

She shook her head. "No, no, I don't think—"

He reached down and grabbed her by the hand, hauling her to her feet. "I insist. And I know you want to."

She did, but suddenly the idea of standing so close to Channing on that board seemed a very bad idea, indeed. And she had the perfect excuse. "Phil—"

"—is not going to win this one," he finished sternly.

"She has to learn that we both can make room in our lives for someone else without losing each other."

Jolie opened her mouth to argue the point but couldn't think of any reason that wasn't purely self-serving. Reluctantly she followed him to the end of the pier, where Phil was rushing to make the board fast. She hopped up just as they reached her and grabbed onto Chan's arm.

"I'm thirsty! Let's have something to drink."

"You go ahead," he said patiently. "I'm rested enough to take Jolie out now."

Phil tugged on him desperately. "Don't you think you've had enough sun for one day? Let's go back to the house."

Jolie sensed the exasperation he was feeling, but he answered as patiently as before. "You're right. I should reapply my sunscreen."

Releasing Jolie, he let Phil tug him back to the table. Picking up the tube of sunscreen from the chair where he'd piled their gear, he began applying it. Phil helped him, rubbing it on his shoulders and back as he slicked down his arms and legs. All the while, she was speaking softly and urgently. When he was done, he turned to face his daughter.

"You did well out there, Phil. I'm proud of you. But I can't like this possessiveness I'm seeing in you. I know you don't think so now, but one day you'll grow up and get married yourself. You'll have a life separate from me. But what of me, Phil? Don't you think I deserve a full life, too?"

Phil stared at him in sheer horror. Then she abruptly whirled and ran away, footsteps pounding on the wharf. Grimly, Channing carried the tube of sunscreen toward Jolie.

"You should go after her," Jolie said.

"No, I don't think so. I've found it best to ignore her when she resorts to this sort of dramatics. Take off that top so I can put some sunscreen on you."

She did as instructed, and he squirted white cream into one hand and began briskly applying it to her back. "I know what she's feeling right now, Chan," Jolie argued, trying to ignore the hot weight of his hands sliding over her bare skin. "She doesn't think anyone will ever w-want her."

He stilled suddenly. "Is that what you thought?" he asked softly.

She felt a sharp pain in her chest. That was what she'd thought, maybe what she still thought, but admitting it was more than she could manage. "She thinks you're the only one who will ever want her around, and that if I come into your life, you'll forget about her."

"She's wrong," he said, filling his hand with lotion once more and going down on one knee to begin slathering her leg. "But the only way to prove her wrong is to show her." Jolie jerked as his hand slid up her leg. "Whoever told you that you have puffy thighs?" he wanted to know.

Jolie answered almost without thought. "My stepmother—one of them."

"She was jealous," he said decisively, skimming his hand up under the hem of her shorts. "You have beautiful legs."

"Thank you," she whispered, concentrating on not trembling as he finished covering her exposed skin with sunscreen. Finished at last, he tossed the tube away and rose to take her by the hand.

"Come on. Let me teach you how to fly on water."

"Chan," she said, beseeching him with tone and look to really hear her, "I'm not what she needs."

"You're exactly what she needs," he countered firmly, "you and I together. You understand her as no one else has ever done except me. You deal with her almost as well as I do already. Do you know how most people react to her, Jo? As soon as she opens her mouth, they recoil in a kind of horror, or they ignore her, pretend she's beneath their regard."

"That's what most adults do with most kids, Chan."

"But it hurts her. It wounds her. I know, I know, she's frightened and hurting now, but she has to learn to open up with someone besides me. We can't give in to her theatrics. She'll take every advantage if we do."

"And what happens when we don't marry, Chan?" Jolie had to ask.

He lifted a hand to her face, cupping her cheek lightly. "I won't worry about that unless you ask it again at the end of our contract."

That time suddenly seemed farther away rather than closer. She wanted to tell him, firmly, that it wouldn't make any difference, but she feared that the words wouldn't come out the way she intended, not with him standing there looking down into her face as if she was the answer to his prayers. She gulped. "I—I just hope you know what you're d-doing—with Phil."

"I do. We won't stay out long, and when we go in, we'll be patient and pleasant and firm. Tell me you don't think that's best."

Jolie closed her eyes. He was right, of course. Blast him, he was always right. She was just feeling so much herself in this moment that she wasn't thinking clearly. She could almost believe that he really did want her for himself. Phil had told her how dangerously convincing he could be, and she realized now that she should have listened. One part of her wanted to run away as Phil had done, and another part of her was beginning to crave his attention just as Phil did. Why couldn't she figure what was best to do?

He strapped her into a vest and had her slip on water socks, then began instructing her. Within minutes they were out on the water, standing front to back, his arms about her as he calmly helped her work the line on the sail. More than once she managed to dump them into the water, but he had them back up and sailing again in no time. Then the last time he stayed in the water and boosted her aboard alone, instructing her to take the board in while he swam ashore. Despite the fact that she had the wind behind her—or perhaps because of it since she kept sailing past the pier—he beat her in and was waiting with an unfolded towel.

"I didn't do nearly as well as Phil," she said, grinning despite herself as she shed the life vest.

"She'll love that," Chan told her, smiling broadly as he toweled her shoulders and back. "You did well, though. You'll be proficient in no time."

"Do you really think so?"

"No doubt of it."

"I'm starving," she said, taking the towel from him and mopping her face and chest. His gaze followed the towel and hung right at breast level.

"So am I," he murmured. Suddenly an alarming change was taking place in her body. It was as if her breasts begged for his attention, swelling and firming, practically thrusting themselves in his face. He lifted his gaze to hers and said with such honesty and feeling that she couldn't possibly mistake his meaning, "But I can wait—a while."

She thought her knees would buckle, until he bent and swept up the top she had discarded earlier, thrusting it at her.

"Come on. You can help me make dinner."

She quickly pulled the top over her head and thrust her arms through the sleeves. He picked up her sandals and turned toward the house. As she hurried along behind him, it occurred to her that, even wet, oily and with dirty feet, she had never felt so feminine and pretty.

* * *

They didn't have to bother about dinner, after all. Phil had taken care of it, calling for pizza and tossing together a creditable salad. If the carrots, radishes and tomatoes were carved into irregular lumps, no one mentioned. If Phil seemed a little desperate to prove to Channing that they didn't need Jolie for anything, certainly not for meals, he seemed oblivious. The evidence of tears on Phil's pugnacious face was enough to make Jolie tuck into the salad with embroidered relish and lavish praise. Chan was more circumspect. Thankfully, Phil seemed to relax as they dined.

Afterward, Jolie excused herself to shower and change. She was on her way back downstairs when something made her stop. It wasn't a big sound, not a crash or even a heavy thud, just a sort of *whump,* as if something soft but weighty had met the wall with more force than might be expected. Jolie stood in the empty hallway and listened, waiting for a repetition. When it came, she knew immediately where it had originated. She bit her lip, then pushed aside doubts and slipped through the open exercise room to the hall in front of Phil's room. The sobs were plainly audible here, the sound of whatever was hitting the wall much more pronounced. If the doors to the exercise room had been closed, however, Jolie would have heard none of it. She lifted her hand to knock, then thought better of it and simply tried the knob. The door swung open softly.

Phil stood in the middle of utter chaos, her long hair rumpled, face blotched. She had thrown pillows and dolls and a few lightweight shoes, clothing, towels, even the scarf off the top of her dresser. Obviously she had chosen "quiet" articles. Just as obviously, she didn't want Chan to know how she was venting her anger and frustration.

"I hate you," she snarled at Jolie, swiping angrily at her tears, "and if you tell him I said it, I'll make you pay."

"I won't tell him," Jolie said lightly, stepping inside and closing the door behind her.

"Get out. Leave me alone."

She should. She knew that she had no business there, but she couldn't seem to make herself walk away from this child. Or her father. "Phil, I want to help. Why don't you tell me—"

"Everything was okay," the girl wailed, "before you came!" She sobbed as if her heart were broken.

Jolie didn't know what to say. Obviously the girl hated her. If this thing had seemed ludicrous before, well, it was even more unworkable now.

"I'm sorry, Phil," she mumbled softly. "I'm sure your father thinks he's doing what's best. He has this crazy notion that I...understand you."

"You don't even know me," Phil snorted skeptically.

"You're right. But..." She shook her head. "I—I think I know how you feel. Every time one of my parents remarried, I wouldn't see them for weeks, sometimes months. It was as if they forgot I existed—until I did something to jog their memories. I failed math once just so the headmistress at my boarding school would send a letter requesting a conference." Phil shot her a look of such contempt that Jolie couldn't help a spurt of laughter. "I know," she said. "That wouldn't work for you. No one would ever believe you could actually fail sixth-grade math."

Phil crossed her arms and reluctantly asked, "You went to boarding school?"

"That's right."

"How come?"

Jolie smiled wanly. "It was just best that way. My parents still can't be in the same room together without trying to draw blood. When I was living with one, I rarely saw the other and when I did, they would battle. I decided to try to control things myself, and boarding school allowed me to schedule their visits so they hardly ever had to deal with each other. It worked pretty well—except when they were in the throes of one of their great passions. Actually, now that I think of it, Channing's approach to marriage isn't all that bad, not compared to the way my parents have gone at it. Not that I have any interest in getting married, mind you."

"'Cause you don't want kids?" Phil ventured in a small voice.

"It's the other way around really," Jolie confided. "I wouldn't mind being a mom. I just don't want to be a wife. And kids really do need two parents."

"I don't," Phil said mulishly.

"Maybe not," Jolie answered, "but then you're the exception, aren't you?"

Phil frowned as if uncertain whether that was a compliment, an insult or a simple statement of fact. She nudged a tumbled doll with one toe.

"Can I help you straighten up?" Jolie offered, but Phil shook her head.

Jolie fought the compulsion to insist and finally turned to go. She couldn't leave without one more word of encouragement, though. "The time will pass. Chan will see he's made a mistake, and that'll be that. You'll see."

Phil said nothing, just stared at her with big, cloudy eyes. Jolie went downstairs with a heavy heart.

It would have been easier for her if she'd been able to maintain that attitude. Unfortunately, Chan proved to be a charming, entertaining companion. They discussed Phil honestly, though Jolie was careful to keep the child's confidence just as she'd promised. She couldn't help the deep swell of compassion that she felt for the girl—or the growing attraction that she was developing for Channing Hawkins.

"I knew you'd have an affinity for her," Channing said confidently after they'd talked for some time. He spread an arm along the back of the couch where they were sitting in the den, and Jolie quelled the urge to move away. He was dangerous, this man, more dangerous than she had realized.

"It's just not that easy," Jolie insisted.

"I know that," he replied smoothly, "but you won't give up on her. You're not the type."

Jolie shook her head. "But marriage, Chan. You don't know what you're asking of me."

"I know better than you do," he argued. "I've been there, remember? And even though she wasn't the right woman, I liked being married. I want that again, but without all the messy emotional junk this time. It'll work. I know it will."

"Not with me," she answered almost pleadingly.

He dropped his arm about her shoulders and scooted close, looking down into her upturned face. "Only with you. I'm convinced of it, Jolie. You're everything I've been looking for." He tapped the end of her nose with a forefinger. "I can make you happy, Jo. Just give me a chance."

"I can't," she whispered. "I don't dare."

He smiled indulgently, and she could see that it was an argument she wasn't going to win. She could do nothing but wait him out—and hope her resolve held true.

"So, how was your weekend?"

Jolie looked around her at the baby clutter covering Benny's office floor and then at her partners once more. She had interrupted something. She wasn't certain how she knew that, but she did. Dessie stood beside Ben, who lounged back in his chair, looking up at her expressionlessly, while Mona banged around in the kneehole of his desk. It was

Dessie who had asked the question. Jolie shrugged nonchalantly.

"Okay. The house is really something. We did a little windsurfing. I got glared at a lot. The kid really hates me." She tried not to grimace as she said it, but wasn't entirely successful. She said nothing of how Channing had charmed the socks off her and how Phil had broken her heart.

Dessie and Ben looked at each other and then at her again, seemingly at a loss for words. That feeling of something amiss intensified into an almost painful uneasiness, as if secrets were wafting about on the air, but that was crazy. What could Ben and Dessie have to keep from her? This was merely the result of a stressful weekend.

"How were your weekends?" she asked, hoping to spark some normalcy. Once again their gazes found each other, then quickly bounced away.

"Fine."

"Nothing much doing. Just your standard weekend."

Jolie tried not to feel suspicion. What secrets could her friends and partners have? They had always shared everything. Why did it suddenly feel as if they weren't?

Dessie folded her arms and sat down on the corner of the desk, looking over her shoulder at Jolie. "So, did Hawkins make any moves on you?"

Jolie felt her face flame. "No." She wasn't about to mention the steamy looks he'd given her—or the way they'd seemed to ignite tiny blazes in her traitorous body. Suddenly she knew what the problem was here. Her. She was the one holding back, and she didn't dare do otherwise. To speak aloud of the contrary feelings that Channing Hawkins evoked in her would make them undeniably real. She dared not let that happen.

"I thought he was supposed to be trying to change your mind," Ben was saying cryptically.

Jolie shook herself to full awareness, wanting nothing so much in that moment as to get away from her friends and this dangerous conversation. "Well, he's doing a poor job of it," she quipped as nonchalantly as possible, preparing to change the subject.

A loud bump from the kneehole was followed by an even louder wail, and Benny was suddenly ratcheting forward to pull Mona from beneath his desk, crooning, "Oh, baby bump her head? Come here, darlin'. Poor baby."

"Uh-oh," Jolie teased, hiding her relief as she quickly backed out of the room, "my cue to cut and run." Just before she turned away, she saw Dessie get up from the desk, walk around behind Benny's chair and lean down, wrapping her arms around both Ben and the little one snuffling against his shoulder. It might have struck her as odd if she hadn't been so grateful for the distraction. At the moment, however, she was too busy convincing herself that Chan Hawkins hadn't gotten to her on some level that past weekend, and that she would do well to simply steer clear of his troublesome daughter until he gave up this ludicrous scheme of his.

Chan pulled into the nearly empty multi-car garage behind his palatial home and killed the truck's engine. He had, of course, expected to see Jolie tonight, but he'd been surprised to find her car already beneath the drive-through. He'd left her a message, after all, saying that he'd be late for their dinner date. Had he realized she would actually be waiting here for him, he'd have hurried—as if he hadn't anyway.

Choosing the door that led along a short corridor to the kitchen, the back stairs and the empty maid's quarters over the garage, he let himself into the kitchen, intending to make his way to the den, where he expected her to be waiting.

Instead, he drew up short, swamped by mouth-watering aromas and the gentle hum of a slightly off-tune voice. He turned his head to find Jolie standing at his stove, his own white bib apron tied around her neck and waist over a tiny coral-colored T-shirt that rode the tops of her hips and dark blue shorts that left a wonderfully indecent amount of bare leg showing. He cocked his head, imagining that apron with frills and ruffles and replacing those shorts and top with…nothing at all. Suddenly his heart was pounding, blood rushing.

Quietly, he slipped up behind her, slid an arm around her waist and dropped his mouth to her ear. She jerked and froze. "That's quite a get-up you're wearing, Miss Winters. What are you doing in my kitchen making your own dinner?"

He felt her muscles twitch, as if she fought the impulse to bolt, but to his surprise she stood her ground, lifted the lid off a heavy pot and stirred it. The aroma nearly knocked him off his feet. His stomach growled. She wedged a haughty look out of the corner of one eye.

"I happen to be a very good cook, thank you very much. I just thought, since you were running late, that this would be quicker than going out. Besides, it's my turn. You've fed me several times now."

He didn't argue. His nose had already convinced him. "Is that beef?"

"With red wine, fresh garlic, onion, bay leaf and cabbage."

"I could eat the smell of it," he said, inhaling deeply.

She chuckled. "You'll have to for another half hour or so."

"In that case, I'll go say hello to my daughter. Any idea where she is?"

A slight pause. "In her room." She turned her head, casting him a speaking look. "Doing homework."

He sighed inwardly. Not very likely, even if the summer course he had allowed her to enroll in at the community college had begun. Phil was just being more stubborn than usual. But she couldn't out-stubborn him, not when he was right, by golly. And Jolie in his arms felt very right. He ducked his head, but Jolie turned just enough so that his kiss landed on her cheek instead of her mouth. She bent forward, industriously tending her pot, and he let her go, bemused by her tactics, pleased that she hadn't pushed away from him.

"I'll be back in a few minutes to help you."

"No hurry," she mumbled.

He turned toward the door.

"Channing?"

He swung around. "Yes?"

"Let her know how important she is to you."

"I always do."

She shook her head. "I know you think you do, but...just make a special effort for a while. Please."

"All right." He didn't point out how motherly that sounded, merely smiled and left the room at a sedate trot, not slowing until he reached his daughter's bedroom.

Phil was sitting at the computer. "Hello, sweetheart. What're you doing?"

She left the keyboard and turned her chair sideways, looking small and girlish and obstinate. "Nothing much. It's a survey for my statistics class."

He lifted an eyebrow. Maybe he'd misjudged her. "Sounds interesting."

She shrugged unenthusiastically. "It's okay."

"Better take a break soon. Jolie's making dinner, and from the smell of it you won't want to be late to the table."

Her jaw jutted out, and she ground her teeth. "I'm not hungry."

He bit back an order and instead wandered over to lower himself gingerly onto the edge of her bed. "Please don't be rude, Phil. I don't want to be cross with you."

"*You* brought her here."

"Jolie has nothing to do with this. You're acting as if she's come between us, but that's not possible, Phil. You're my daughter. I love you."

To his surprise, she hurled herself out of her chair and into his arms. "I'm sorry, Chan. I love you, too. I don't mean to be this way. I know it's stupid, but I can't help it."

"It's all right, sweetheart. Just do your best, and everything will work out. You'll see. No more tears now. Everything's fine."

She slipped down to sit by his side, and he smoothed her long, luxurious hair with his hands, smiling. "How was your day?"

She sighed and hitched up a shoulder. "Same old same old. The other students ignore me. The teachers treat me like some sort of lab experiment gone awry. At least the class discussion was more interesting than regular school."

They chatted about the limo service he had hired to get her from place to place and the female driver he had specified. He disliked leaving Phil on her own, but the elderly "companion" they'd employed for the past two years had retired, and Phil had not found a replacement to her liking. He knew that she was smart enough not to do anything physically risky, but she was still a little girl, and he couldn't help worrying, despite numerous phone calls throughout the day. Community college was a recent compromise since she'd tried and disliked day camp. He made a mental note to discuss the situation with Jolie. She certainly seemed to understand Phil on a visceral level.

They chatted a while longer before he went to change clothes and rejoin Jolie downstairs. He found her in the process of laying the table in the breakfast room.

"Here, let me do that."

She placed a plate in the center of a straw place mat and shrugged. "You can clean up."

"Deal." He reached for and placed the flatware.

"Hope you don't mind me making myself familiar with your kitchen," she said, folding napkins.

"Not at all. What I hope is that it will be your kitchen, too, soon."

She clucked her tongue and shook her head. "Chan, you're a very nice man, and I like you. I'm sure you'd make a fine husband, and if I were inclined to marry, I would seriously consider you. But I'm not, and I can't."

"Are you sure about that? Seems to me you fit in real well around here."

"Phil doesn't think so."

"Phil doesn't know *what* she's thinking right now."

"Well, I'm not Phil, and I know my own mind."

"Is that so? Care to put it to the test?"

She spluttered with cryptic laughter. "I hope you're not proposing a trial marriage."

"Nothing so drastic," he said, moving around the table toward her. She seemed to sense at the last moment what he had in mind and stepped around a chair, effectively putting it between them. Very casually, he slid out his foot and shoved the chair away, saying, "A kiss should be sufficient."

She drew up small when he reached for her but did not back away. "Chan," she said pleadingly, her voice roughened and breathless, "don't."

He stepped close, sliding his hands down her slender back

to her waist and pulled her against him. "Why? Afraid of the outcome?"

"No. I—I just don't see the point."

He curled a finger under her chin and lifted her face. "The point is," he said, finding it true, "I very much want to kiss you." And he did, settling his mouth over hers with infinite care. She had fisted her hands against his chest, but as he employed his mouth, gently coaxing her to respond, her hands unfurled and flattened. Encouraged, he parted his lips and licked against the seam of her mouth. She made a small sound that might have signified acceptance or hunger or frustration, and then she opened for him, her arms sliding up and around his neck.

He plunged into her, desire and triumph roaring through him. His arms wrapped around her, seeking full-body contact. The weight of her breasts against his chest inflamed him, the fit of her pelvis against his, the long, creamy length of her thighs. Oh, how he would love to feel those legs wrap around him, to throw aside clothing and constraints and doubts and take this woman to bed. Soon, he promised himself. Soon.

Chapter Seven

Sensation swirled around Jolie, lifting and lightening her. Yet, a strange, strong heat kept her anchored, holding at bay the fear that she might float apart and away, allowing her to enjoy with stunned concentration the reactions of her own body. Hard, soft, swelling, firmness, moisture, fluid. Elation. She felt caught up in a dream, swirling among the clouds. With Chan. A buzzing gradually penetrated her consciousness. She tried to shut it out, but it irritated, reality beckoning.

Suddenly she was alone, spiraling pell-mell toward earth. She opened her eyes and looked up into Channing's scowling face. It was then that she realized what she was doing; how she was standing pressed against him, on tiptoe, her arms wrapped about his neck so tightly that it was a wonder he could breathe. Gasping, she jerked away, aware of two things simultaneously. He had proved his point, and her dinner was burning.

"The timer!"

"I'll get it," he said gruffly, hurrying toward the kitchen.

She followed him, hovering and watching anxiously as he first turned off the gas burner and then the buzzer. He lifted off the lid.

"Is it all right?"

"Looks fine to me."

She breathed a sigh of relief, but when he turned back to her, she saw instantly that he was not thinking of food—unless she was dessert! Her bones turned to liquid. She had to grasp the counter to stay upright. He stepped toward her, and she lifted a hand to ward him off, as if she could manage such a thing.

"I think we should revise our agreement," he said huskily, sweeping a melting gaze over her.

"M-my dinner," she burbled. "D-don't want...get cold."

"In a minute," he said, reaching for her.

She knew instinctively that if he got his hands on her again, dinner wouldn't be the only thing ruined. Her resolve was nothing more than a mound of ash now. She bolted, uncaring that it was cowardly and blatantly telling. "I-I'll get Phil," she called over her shoulder.

He growled something that she was quite certain she didn't want to hear, so she ignored it, not stopping until she reached the turret and the stairwell. There she put her back to the wall and tried to stiffen her shaking legs.

Dear heaven, what had he done to her? What had she allowed him to do? She'd known this was a bad idea tonight. Why hadn't she listened to that little voice warning her of trouble? Phil. The idea of Phil beckoned like a fire in a snowstorm, warm reality in a world of cold sensation. A moment with the girl who hated and rejected her would restore her equilibrium and good sense. She climbed and approached the bedroom door.

Jolie tapped, heard nothing, tapped again. After the third

try, she opened the door and walked in. Phil was at the computer, eyes fixed to the screen, fingers flying over the keyboard. She didn't even look up when Jolie stepped into the room.

"Dinner's ready," Jolie said, bracing herself for the usual invective.

Phil ignored her.

"Aren't you hungry? Your dad is, I'm sure. He's had a long day."

Phil grimaced. "In a minute. This is the good part."

Encouraged—and still craven enough to be stalling for time to gather her wits—Jolie strolled toward the computer desk. "What are you working on?"

Phil paused in typing and shot Jolie a smug, disdainful glance. "Nothing you'd be interested in." When she turned her gaze back to the computer screen, she spluttered a chuckle and once more began tapping away. Curious, Jolie stepped around behind her and began to read.

Anyone at the Red Dog last night?

What happened? Someone mentioned a virgin rumple? Explain please.

They got it on in the middle of the floor with everyone watching!! You could see everything!

Jolie goggled. "What is this?"

Phil whirled around in her chair and leapt up to her feet, blocking Jolie's view. "None of your business! Get away!"

But Jolie knew that she couldn't do that. She darted around Phil and quickly scanned the screen, picking up where she'd left off.

It's an initiation dare. All the virgins who want to pledge put their names in a jar—male/female. And they draw one each. If they get yours you have to do it in front of everybody.

Did they take off their clothes?

Every stitch, and they had to drink a bunch of booze first.

Phil reached around Jolie and hit a button. The computer screen went black. "You have no right—" she began, but Jolie was too alarmed to listen.

"That was a chat room, one you had no business being in! Does your father know you're doing this?" Phil shoved out her chin mutinously, but Jolie saw the glimmer of fear in the owlish eyes behind those thick glasses. Of course, he didn't know! Jolie put her hand to her head. What was she going to do with this child? And she *was* a child, far too young to be involved in something like—virgin rumples? She grabbed Phil by the hand. "We're going downstairs, young lady. You're going to tell your father just what you've been up to."

"I don't have to go anywhere with you!" Phil cried, yanking free to throw herself onto the bed.

"Oh, yes, you do," Jolie said flatly. "You can walk under your own power or I'll drag you, but you are going downstairs to talk to your father."

Phil glared, then wobbled her chin and, when that didn't work, actually shed real tears. Jolie's heart turned over, and she knew at once what was happening. Chan was so right about the theatrics!

"Up," she ordered, folding her arms. "Or I'll just go get Chan and bring him here."

Frowning, Phil got up off the bed. Then suddenly she bolted from the room. Obviously she meant to get to Chan first. Jolie shook her head. She had to hand it to the girl; she had a far wider repertoire than Jolie had imagined. Grimly, Jolie started after her.

She heard the sobbing propaganda long before she reached the breakfast nook.

"She hates me! I was just talking to my friends. Can't I even have my own friends?"

Chan was obviously confused. He looked up from Phil's teary face, his hands on her heaving shoulders. "What on earth is going on?"

Jolie leaned a shoulder against the door frame and folded her arms. "I caught her in an on-line chat room. They were discussing something called a virgin rumple."

Chan's eyes went wide. He looked down at Phil. "Please tell me that isn't what I think it is."

Phil shrugged unconvincingly. "I don't know what it is."

"If she didn't before, she does now," Jolie informed him evenly. "It was fully explained. And not by nine-year-olds."

Phil rolled her eyes. "The dean told you we'd be discussing mature themes," she said.

"In the classroom, under the guidance of an instructor," Channing said, "not on-line!"

Phil pulled away from him, her face set in a familiar, stubborn mask. "What difference does it make? She's just trying to make trouble."

"You made this trouble, Phil," Chan said, "not Jo."

"How old do they think you are?" Jolie asked, hoping to keep the discussion focused where it belonged. Phil pulled out a chair and plopped down in it, shrugging.

"What does it take to get into this chat room, Phil?" Channing demanded.

She gripped the curved arms of the chair and mumbled, "Just a student ID number."

"In other words, they think you're college age, eighteen or nineteen, at least. Right? I knew this college thing was a bad idea. You're withdrawn as of Monday morning."

"Chan!"

"And your Internet access is cut."

Phil came to her feet. "My computer—"

"You can keep the computer," he interrupted firmly,

"but the phone line is gone until I'm confident you won't or can't do something this inappropriate again."

"I was just trying to make friends!" she screamed. "You don't even want me to have friends!"

"You know that's not true."

"It's not a real friendship, Phil, if they don't even know how old you are," Jolie pointed out gently, but Phil was already tearing out of the room. Chan went after her, demanding first that she walk and second that she wait for him in her room. Phil walked stiff-legged toward the foyer and the stairs, trembling with emotion. Jolie sighed, and slumped against the wall. Chan massaged his temples with his fingertips as he returned to her.

"I never dreamed... She's so damned lost. The poor kid doesn't have a friend in the world."

"Too mature for those her own age and too young for those she's attempting to cultivate," Jolie said softly.

"I've tried every way I know to help her fit in," he went on. "And this is just the tip of the iceberg. Dear God, can you imagine what puberty is going to be like for her? It's more than I can handle alone."

"I'm sorry, Chan," Jolie whispered. "I'm so sorry."

"It's not your fault," he said, reaching for her hands. "You did the right thing. No telling what harm she could come to if we hadn't found out."

"I don't mean that. I mean, for Phil. Just imagine what it's like to have no friends. No wonder she's so hostile. She's afraid of losing you, of being rejected by me and everyone else she meets."

"Now do you see how much we need you?" he asked softly, squeezing her hands.

They needed someone, but her? On the other hand, who else was there? Dismayed but resigned, Jolie nodded mutely. Channing stepped close and gathered her against him.

"Thank you," he whispered. "Thank you."

She stood for a moment within the comforting welcome of his arms, then gently stepped away. "I'm only agreeing to help Phil," she said. "A few lessons in socialization, a new friend or two. She has to learn how to be a kid."

He looked for a moment as if he would argue, but then he smiled wanly and lifted a hand to cup her cheek. "I suppose beggars can't be choosers," he said softly. "Do whatever you can for her. God knows I've tried everything I can think of. Whatever you do, I'll appreciate it. And I'll try to let that be enough—for now."

It was a disaster. Jolie sat in the booth and watched it unfold, cold pizza congealing on the table. Phil had pitched a fit when told about the outing, but Chan had held firm, and in the end she had risen to the occasion. No, this catastrophe must be laid unequivocally at Jolie's own door. She never should have invited two strange girls to lunch. They were off together now, giggling and whispering as they pretended to try their hands at miniature bowling, while Phil glumly studied the patterns and variations of a video game played by the father of two toddlers. When the man's turn was done, he smacked the machine disgustedly with the palm of one hand and walked away, dragging his little ones with him. Phil stepped up, slipped her tokens into the machine and studiously set about racking up a shockingly high score. What she lacked in physical speed and reflexes, she made up for with lightning-quick decisions and amazingly astute deductions. And not a soul noticed except for Jolie. She got up and walked over to the game, intending to lend support and voice judicious praise, only to have Phil abruptly abandon the machine, stomp back to the booth and plop down.

Jolie's heart ached. She had tried. Phil had really tried, and Jolie had seen what it had cost her, but the girls knew that she wasn't like them. Jolie had not told them or her parents about Phil other than to say that she was bored now that school was out and that her father was at a loss how to entertain her. Yet, the girls had sensed that Phil was not like them, that her too-bright smiles and silences were uncharacteristic and masked something far deeper than the average nine-year-old could understand. Jolie wished she'd paid more attention to the girls over the years that she'd socialized with their parents. Perhaps she would have realized how this would turn out.

She wandered over to the booth, trying not to be hurt that Phil obviously wanted to avoid her company as much as the other girls wanted to avoid Phil's.

"Want another slice of pizza?"

Phil shook her head, long hair rippling.

"How about some dessert?"

Phil folded her arms. "I just want to go home."

Jolie sighed inwardly, but she couldn't blame the girl. She dropped a hand on Phil's shoulder and felt her flinch. "I'll get the others," she said, quickly turning away.

"She tried so hard," Jolie said morosely, "but as good an actress as she is—and, believe me, she has a natural theatricality—she just couldn't mask that formidable intelligence. I shouldn't have asked her to try, not that I realized that was what I was doing."

Dessie shook her head. "Poor kid. She must feel like a true misfit."

"And I sure didn't help," Jolie admitted.

"But you tried, and that's important," Dessie assured her. "If she's as smart as you say she is, she'll realize that."

"But it doesn't solve her problem, does it?" Jolie retorted. She sighed in apology. "Sorry. Didn't mean to snap. It's just that I'm so frustrated. How do you teach a kid smart enough to grasp quantum mathematics what it means to play? That's really the problem. She doesn't know how to enjoy herself in any way that others her own age can relate to."

Dessie shrugged. "Try using her natural talents. You say she has a gift for theatrics. Maybe an acting class would open up some possibilities."

Jolie was not enthusiastic, but she didn't have any better ideas. She decided that she might as well make some calls to find out what was available. The only thing she came up with that was currently available was a parent/child workshop, but when she broached the subject with Channing, he made it clear that he wouldn't have the time for late-afternoon classes. With the launch of the newly dubbed Hawk looming, he had his hands full at the office. Dessie and Ben were swamped, too, so much so that Jolie was feeling a little useless now that her part in securing the account was finished. She had a few irons in the fire, of course, but nothing that was going to overheat until the Hawk campaign hit. As much as she disliked casting herself in the role of parent, she really had no good reason not to try this with Phil.

Phil was not exactly enthusiastic herself, but as before Channing really gave her no choice in the matter, and despite an awkward start that had them both explaining their non-relationship repeatedly, the class proved to be genuine fun. At first, Phil couldn't get past the sheer silliness of some of the exercises, but once the activities deepened, she proved herself a truly gifted thespian. Her startlingly accurate memory, keen observations and, of course, that mammoth intelligence served her well. She showed a clear preference for drama, but also displayed a surprisingly wry sense of humor. If she didn't exactly make friends with the other kids in the class, she didn't make enemies, either, and when the instructors assigned group projects, everyone wanted to be on Phil's team.

Phil, naturally, volunteered her home as rehearsal space, and a quick call to Channing confirmed that he had no objections—quite the reverse, in fact. He was delighted, and he made sure that Jolie knew it, showering her with praise and affection. Jolie was relieved when Phil banned him from the troupe's meetings, but that didn't keep Chan from showing up at her office or apartment during the next weeks, wagging flowers and chocolates and small, sentimental gifts that Jolie had to fight hard to remind herself had no real significance.

Phil, meanwhile, was in her element. After much discussion, the troupe decided that they would perform an old-fashioned melodrama. Given only twenty minutes of performance time and ten minutes for staging, they agreed to forgo trying to condense a published play in preference for writing their own. Phil was brilliant at pulling together the ideas tossed out by the others into one workable premise. They borrowed a laptop from Channing, and Jolie went to work with the only dad in the group writing it all down. Soon they'd come up with a fun premise that had everyone laughing and blurting out possible lines. Phil volunteered to put it into a script, and the first meeting finished up with cold canned sodas and cookies which Jolie had purchased from a bakery downtown. Channing was allowed to join them, but Phil insisted that he be told nothing of the plans they were making. Clearly she wanted to surprise him on the night of the performance.

That night came all too quickly for Jolie's peace of mind. They were restricted to scenery and props that they could borrow or make with what was on hand. No one was allowed to buy anything and all donations had to be made to the workshop as a whole. Given those parameters, they were reduced to painting bed sheets as backdrops and constructing cardboard edifices. Costuming proved easy enough since they were using a Western theme, but Phil had to be happy with a Mexican sombrero since none of the available cowboy hats were large enough to cover her wealth of bundled-up hair. Jolie herself got stuck playing an unlikely wooden Indian who came to life only to comment on the goings-on of the "real" characters. The role required her to be on stage the entire time and to stand frozen during most of it, and Jolie couldn't help feeling that Phil had maneuvered her into it as a sort of punishment, a statement of her undying enmity, but it was a small price to pay for watching Phil actually enjoying herself.

By the time performance night rolled around, the fun had disappeared in a flutter of nerves for everyone. Jolie tried to be a calming influence, but the butterflies in her own stomach made it difficult. Phil, on the other hand, was a true grouch, grumbling about everyone and everything. When her hair tumbled down for the fourth time before she could get the sombrero jammed down on top of it, she actually threw her brush across the dressing room of the community center where they were performing and yanked on the long, blond tresses, declaring, "I hate this mop!"

"Surely not," Jolie said mildly, going after the brush. "You have such beautiful hair."

"Some day I'm going to cut it, no matter what Chan says," Phil insisted mulishly. "It's hot, and it takes forever to brush."

Jolie found another rubber band and went to work pulling

Phil's hair up on top of her head and securing it with pins. "I'm sure Channing would let you cut your hair if you really wanted to," she commented.

"No, he wouldn't," Phil insisted. "I've tried and tried to get him to, but he wants me to keep it long." She made a face and wiggled her upper lip, testing her glued-on handlebar mustache for stability. Thoughtfully, Jolie fitted the hat down over the mountain of hair piled atop the girl's head. Phil tightened the string, looked herself over, then removed her glasses. Leaning close to the mirror, she took stock again, then nodded and got up. Whipping a toy six-gun from the holster on her hip, she shoved it from beneath her serape at Jolie's midsection, and in her best Mexican accent quipped, "I thinks you goin' to die, Black Bart."

"I thinks you goin' to be a spectacular José José Sanchez Santiago Jones," Jolie replied, and Phil laughed, returning her gun to the holster.

"If I don't stumble over the scenery or shoot the wrong actor."

"You can see well enough without your glasses to manage."

Phil hitched up a shoulder in a show of nonchalance. "It's just a dumb old play, not a major motion picture or anything."

"So it is," Jolie agreed lightly. "Now, if you'll excuse me, I have to get into my own costume."

Phil shrugged again and wandered away. While she slathered on her make-up and wrestled with the ratty, shellacked wig she had to wear, Jolie noticed that Phil spent her time going over lines with the skinny seven-year-old playing Black Bart. The kid was nervous at the best of times, and he looked positively ill tonight, despite his mother's most soothing attentions. The woman had confessed to Jolie that she was hoping to help her son overcome his shyness, and

Jolie had passed that information to Phil. Ever since, Phil had taken pains to encourage the boy. Jolie smiled at the laughable reflection of herself smeared with dark grease paint and wearing black braids. She made a mental note to thank Dessie, who would be in the audience, for coming up with this scheme.

The families and friends of the performers filled only a small section of the folding seats set up for the audience, but they were an enthusiastic lot, whistling and stomping their feet in addition to applauding. Jolie both regretted inviting Dessie and Ben and felt grateful for having someone of her own in the audience. At least Mona's restlessness didn't upset or disturb anyone, as she was just one of a number of toddlers and infants present and the atmosphere was supremely informal.

When it came time to set the makeshift stage for their performance, all the cast had to pitch in to get it done in time, but Phil had everything so well organized that it went without a hitch. Then it was time to take their places and wait for the curtain, which was nothing more than a black plastic sheet strung on clothesline, to part.

It was Phil who set the tone, playing her role with such aplomb and enjoyment that no one else could help having a good time. She prompted Black Bart whenever he faltered and stepped in with fresh lines to clarify the muddle that twelve-year-old Penelope made of her part at one point, and in the end it was Phil and her "horse," the lone dad in the troupe, who garnered the lion's share of the cheers.

Jolie felt flush with triumph. She had remembered all of her lines and managed to elicit a few laughs from the audience. It was not her performance that elated her but, rather, Phil's. Some of Jolie's enthusiasm waned, however, when Chan strolled up with her friends, baby Mona parked on his hip as if she belonged there. His parents were with them and heaped effusive praise on Phil and gratitude on Jolie, who could only cringe at meeting them for the first time dressed as a wooden Indian. Most disturbing of all, though, was the way Phil warmed up to Dessie.

The girl positively gushed over Mona and treated Dessie like a favorite aunt, all but ignoring Jolie. If not for Channing, Jolie might have faded into the background for all the others seemed to notice. As it was, however, once he had captured her hand and pulled her over to meet his parents, he never let it go again, even when Mona started climbing him like a jungle gym and wound up sitting on his left shoulder, from which vantage point she could keep her right foot in his face. He just laughed, nibbled her ankle and caught her with one hand when she tumbled off in a fit of giggles.

Someone suggested that the troupe go out for a celebratory ice cream cone, sending everyone back to the dressing room to change and clean up. Phil was one of the first ones changed, but she sat brushing out her hair while everyone else caught up with her. Occasionally she yanked or growled at knots that had worked their ways into the ends of her hair. Jolie decided that she would speak to Channing. The girl really did need a trim at least.

The opportunity came as they were sitting in a booth at the ice cream parlor, Dessie and Ben across the table from them, Channing's parents and Phil in the booth behind. Jolie could hear Phil going on and on to her doting grandparents about the play and the workshop. As long as the ice cream lasted, Mona was content to sit in her mother's lap and eat, but once Dessie's supply was exhausted, Mona decided to crawl across the table to Chan and Jolie. Chan scooped the baby up and stood her between them, one hand clamped firmly over her little tummy while Jolie spooned the remainder of her own ice cream into the toddler's ever-open mouth. Talk continued unabated for a time, then Dessie decided to visit the ladies' room while Ben returned to the service counter for a soft drink. It was then that Channing once again captured Jolie's hand in his and looked at her over the top of Mona's bobbing head.

"You've made my daughter very happy," he said softly. "Just listen to her."

Jolie couldn't help smiling. "I have been." He squeezed her hand, and opened his mouth to say something more, a soft light in his bright blue eyes. Sensing that she wouldn't like what he was about to say, she beat him to it. "I have a couple of thoughts about Phil if you don't mind listening."

He stared a moment, then nodded brusquely. "Go ahead."

"I think you should look for a formal acting class for her, perhaps something connected to the community theatre scene. I discovered a class that starts in about another week."

"Sounds good. I'll get the information from you and discuss it with her."

Mona gave a little hop then, nearly bashing Channing in the face, and flopped over into his lap. He wrestled her around into a sitting position.

"One more thing," Jolie went on, keeping her voice pitched low.

He looked up expectantly. "Yes?"

"You really ought to let her cut her hair."

His eyebrows shot up. "Oh, no. We've been over this. Phil knows—"

"It's *her* hair, Chan," Jolie argued. "How would you like it if someone else told you how to wear yours?"

He paused, then shook his head. "It's not the same."

"Why isn't it?"

"It's just not."

"I can't believe you're being so stubborn about this," Jolie said. "Do you have any idea how difficult it is to wash, rinse, dry and comb hair the length of hers? Do you know how hot it gets, especially this time of year?"

Doubt was creeping into his eyes, but he remained adamant. "She can put it up."

"Do you know how difficult that is? It's too much for a young girl."

"But that's exactly it," Channing confessed, leaning forward to keep from being overheard. "She's a girl, and frankly, her hair is the only thing that's at all girlish about her. If she gives that up—"

"That's so not true!" Jolie exclaimed, wincing at the realization that she was overheard. She leaned forward, one elbow braced on the table top, and lowered her voice. "Cutting her hair won't make Phil any less of a girl. And if you're so worried about that, why did you stick her with a boy's nickname?"

"I didn't. She did that herself. And I let her because at the time it was cute and I didn't want her to deny or forget her origins," he said, adding, "Donnelly Phillips deserved that much consideration from both of us."

"Then look at it this way, being called Phil doesn't make her any less a girl, does it? Why should cutting her hair do that?"

Channing sighed and removed a napkin from Mona's mouth and hands. "Do you really think I ought to let her cut it?"

"Yes."

He grimaced, obviously wrestling with the problem.

"Look," Jolie said, "there's lots of room for compromise here. She doesn't have to cut it all off. She could cut a good foot off it and still have lots of hair to put in a ponytail or braid."

He still hesitated, so Jolie pulled out her trump card.

"My hair's short," she pointed out. "Does it make me any less feminine?"

He narrowed his eyes. "Don't be absurd." Suddenly he leaned toward her until their noses were almost touching and whispered, "You could shave your head and still make my blood boil, if you want to know."

She didn't. And yet, some small, perverse part of her thrilled to the knowledge. Swallowing, she sat back, putting distance between them.

"I don't know what that has to do with anything," she said. Then, determined to win on this one, she lifted her chin and stated, "I'm going to make an appointment with a stylist. You can come with us, if you want."

He frowned and rubbed a hand over his face, only to have Mona lift her little hands and repeat the procedure for him until he smiled. "Okay, okay, but I'm not liking this."

"You'll get over it," Jolie said with satisfaction. "Besides, if you really hate it, all you have to do is wait for it to grow out again."

"Oh, sure," he quipped doubtfully, "nine more years."

"It wouldn't take that long," she assured him, grinning broadly. "Go ahead and tell her. I want to see her face when you do."

Sighing in the most put-upon fashion, Channing set Mona on her feet again and twisted around to look over his shoulder. Jolie did the same. Phil looked up from across the booth behind them when he called her name. Channing cut a look at Jolie, then baldly announced, "Jolie's going to make you an appointment to have your hair cut."

Phil's mouth fell open. Her grandmother—a thin, patrician-looking woman with short, silver-gray hair—gasped, clapped her hands and reached across the table. Phil gave one hand to her grandmother and lifted the other to the top of her head. "Really?" she breathed.

The look Channing slid Jolie this time contained a smile. "Really," he confirmed, adding, "but not too short."

Phil looked at her grandmother, eyebrows raised in an expression of enduring shock, and the two laughed while Channing's bull-built father looked on indulgently. Jolie had noticed earlier that Chan seemed to have more in common with his mother's looks than his father's, but she saw something of the latter's mannerisms in Channing now. The way he smiled, the warm glow of affection in his eyes, an air of indulgent authority, even the way he tilted his head when listening or thinking. The two men glanced at each other, and in that instant they communicated a world of understanding. Jolie could see Phil and Channing trading that look in a few years, and the thought gladdened her heart, but it also saddened her because she knew without a shred of doubt that she would never enjoy the same with her parents. Somehow, they simply did not connect, but for the first time, Jolie seriously suspected that the fault was not hers.

What must it be like to live with such assurance, such acceptance, such intimacy? A yearning that she hadn't felt for years opened a place in her that she had thought forever closed. She hadn't understood it before, but she did now. It was the need to be fully and completely known, accepted and loved.

Oh, yes, Phil was having a difficult time of it now, and perhaps she would for some time to come, but in the end Phil would have what Jolie had never had and never could. Or could she?

She stared unabashedly as the hands of Chan's parents crept together, drawn, it seemed, without true awareness on the part of either, a tangible sharing in a small moment of excitement, hope and triumph for a loved one. It was a minor action taken in one of life's smaller moments, and yet it bespoke a huge, encompassing togetherness. Was she wrong to feel something of the same when Channing's hand settled upon her shoulder, effectively trapping baby Mona between them? Her natural instinct was denial, but suddenly she remembered something a philosophy professor had once said in a lecture. A failure to believe does not make a fact less true.

Was it possible that marriage could be much more than she had believed? And could Channing Hawkins be the one right husband in all the world for her?

Chapter Eight

"We have an appointment," Jolie said, as Channing followed her and Phil into the pink-and-chrome reception area. The heavily made-up girl at the reception desk shoved a tiny set of earphones off her head and left them draped around her neck, where they blared rock music tinnily. She bobbed her multi-colored head in time to the music even as she spoke.

"All three of you?"

"Er, no, just her." Jolie pointed at Phil, who was studying the girl's spiked hair with obvious interest. Channing's confidence plummeted, not that it had been very high to begin with. The girl waved at a door draped with a beaded curtain.

"Go on back."

Jolie forged ahead, Phil at her heels. Channing nodded at the bobbing head behind the desk and followed grimly.

"I'm not so sure about this," he hissed at Jolie as he caught up to her in a bright yellow hallway flanked by small dressing rooms.

"Will you relax," she whispered back. "This salon has an excellent reputation."

Just then a small, dark man appeared, throwing his arms wide in welcome.

"*Bueno,* my dears. This way, if you please. I'm Chico."

Jolie smiled as she stepped into the styling room, and Chico immediately started pawing her head and clucking his tongue. "Ooh, girl, you need shaping up real bad."

"I'm, uh, not your client."

"I know," he said with a disheartened sigh. "That would be the baby girl, Dessie said. But I just know that Simon would love to get at you. He's not taking appointments today, but he's here. Why don't I just give him a call?"

Jolie shook her head at the ebullient, chatty man. "I'm just here to support my friend Phil." So saying, she grabbed Phil by the hand and pulled her forward.

According to Dessie, this Chico and his partner Simon operated one of the better shops in Austin, claiming a select clientele, including Dessie herself, who had been letting the duo cut her hair since she'd arrived in Austin as a college freshman. Lately, she'd been trading her advertising expertise for their service, and the outcome had been so much business that she'd had to call in favors to get this appointment for Phil. Channing only hoped that her confidence in the pair was not misplaced. At least Chico didn't make any comments about Phil's masculine name. Apparently he cared only about her hair.

"Girl, you have amazing hair," he announced, plucking at long locks of it. "You just got too much of it." He stepped back, whirled an electric-blue chair and patted the leather seat. "Hop up here and let me have a look at that head. Mm-mm-mm." Whipping off the elastic headband, he filled his hands with Phil's hair. Looking up at Channing in the mirror, Chico shook his own long locks and smiled beneath his pencil-thin mustache. "You must be the protective papa who doesn't want his little girl's hair butchered."

Channing was at his most uncomfortable. He was still uncertain about this, and he'd accepted Jolie's invitation to accompany them in something of a panic, hoping against hope that he could talk them out of this. He saw now what a pipe dream that notion was. Clearing his throat, he nodded. "That's my daughter," he admitted. "I love her hair."

Phil rolled her eyes. Chico fluffed her hair, saying, "Well, you're gonna love it even more when I'm through with it. And more importantly, so will she. Okay, darlin', come with me, and we'll get you changed and washed. Miss Jolie, I'm calling Simon up here."

Jolie was shaking her head again when Chico herded Phil through yet another beaded curtain. Channing slid his hands into the pockets of his pants and looked around him. Exposed pipes and vents overhead had been chromed, shining brightly against a black ceiling. Shocking-pink walls and electric-blue chairs smacked the eye. A bank of lights over a wall of mirrors glared coldly. It was basic and outrageous at the same time. A rich voice crooned in Spanish in the background, competing only minimally with the distant sound of rock and roll on the other side of the wall.

"Let's sit down," Jolie suggested, gesturing toward a small leather couch draped with a fringed shawl. "It'll take some time to wash and rinse that hair."

Channing walked over to the couch with her, waited until she was seated, then tugged up his pants legs and sat. He couldn't help fidgeting. The atmosphere of this place was utterly foreign to him, and he didn't want his daughter's hair cut. It felt as if he was losing a part of her that he'd struggled mightily to hold. Still, if Jolie really thought it was best.... He opened his mouth to question her one more time, but the sudden arrival of a tall, slender, African-

American male with braids and gold hoops in his earlobes locked the questions away permanently.

"Hon*ey!*" The man clapped his long, slender hands together and bowed slightly from the waist, feet turned out, heels together, as he exclaimed, "Simon *has* arrived, and, *oh, my,* not a *moment* too *soon.* I *have* a haircut *perfect* for *you.*" Without warning, he turned on Channing, thrust one of those long, skinny hands at him— "Hel*lo.* How *do* you *do?*"

Completely taken aback, Channing managed to get a hand up to shake and muttered, "Channing Hawkins."

Simon held his hand much too long. "Ooh, he *don't* want *me* messin' with *you,* girl."

Channing yanked his hand away and shot to his feet, thoroughly disgruntled. "So I like my girls the way they are!" he shouted. "Sue me!"

Simon had the nerve to laugh. "That *baby* back *there,*" he said, continuing to stress every other word in an irritating sing-song, "she's *got* what *we* call '*Daddy* hair' '*cause* it's *always* the *daddys* that *don't* want it *touched.*"

Channing rolled his eyes and thrust a finger at Jolie. "She hasn't got 'Daddy hair.'"

Simon considered a moment, one long hand folded languidly beneath his chin. "No, *she's* got *scraggly* hair."

"She does not!" Channing insisted, but Simon ignored him and held out his hand to Jolie.

"Come on, now. You know I'm right. He'll love it, I guarantee."

Channing blinked. The sing-song had disappeared.

"Did Dessie put you up to this?" Jolie demanded.

"Have you ever known our Dessie to be wrong?" Simon returned smoothly.

"She married John, didn't she?"

Simon winced exaggeratedly, then as quickly recovered.

"Well, *she* isn't *wrong* this *time.* Besides, *what* better *way* to *show* your *support?* Or *don't* you *trust* us?"

Channing folded his arms, preparing to tell Simon a thing or two, but then Jolie sighed and resignedly gave Simon her hand. Channing's mouth fell open as she allowed Simon to pull her up and off the couch.

"Jolie!" he protested, but she placed her palm in the center of his chest as she moved past him.

"He's right. I wouldn't trust Phil to someone I wouldn't trust myself to. Just relax."

"I'll *have* someone *bring* you a *glass* of *wine,*" Simon said, leading Jolie away.

"I don't need a glass of wine," Channing grumbled, knowing that he was making mountains out of molehills but somehow unable to stop himself. He liked Jolie's hair. He liked Phil's hair. And he didn't like watching Jolie walk out of the room with another man, even one as silly as Simon. He shoved his hands into his pockets again and jingled his change, then sat down once more and tried to relax. After a few moments, the receptionist brought him a glass of white wine, which he grudgingly accepted before she bobbed away again, refitting her earphones and turning up the tiny radio strapped around her waist.

The wine was surprisingly good. He'd downed half the glass before Phil returned with Chico, chattering like a magpie—a magpie in a black kimono that hung to her ankles and a white towel wound around her head. Chico produced a thick pad and popped it into the seat of the chair. Phil hiked herself up on top of it and went on talking without drawing breath.

"A mustache," she was saying, "a real stiff one with curved ends. I liked it. If I was a guy, I'd grow one."

Chico wiggled his own pencil-thin version and said to his reflection in the mirror, "I *love* facial hair."

"Chan, why don't you grow a mustache?" Phil asked, turning a look over one shoulder.

He shrugged, frowned and sipped his wine, beginning to feel more mellow. "Never thought much about it."

"Oh, I adore this child," Chico gushed. "She's amazing." He shoved her back in the chair, spun it around and brought his hands together against either side of her neck. He jiggled his hands. "Right there. No, no." He jiggled some more, raising and lowering, finally announcing triumphantly, "There!" With that he whipped out a pair of scissors and a comb. The next thing Channing knew, hair was falling. Panic rushed in, but it was too late to stop the cutting now. He threw back the remainder of his wine just as Jolie was ushered into the room by Simon.

She, too, was dressed in a black kimono, but hers rode several inches above her knees. Channing's frown deepened. Jolie smiled and allowed herself to be placed in the chair next to Phil. "I still think it's too curly," she said.

"It *is* not," Simon insisted. "It'll *just* need a *little* gel. You'll *see.*"

When he pulled out a straight razor, Channing flinched. Deciding that he just couldn't watch, he bowed his head and buried his face in his hands, blotting out even the conversation going on around him. Presently, the whirr of a blow-dryer pulled his gaze upward. Simon had finished with Jolie already and was blasting her head with warm air while pulling at her hair with his free hand. Channing watched the hairstyle take shape, marveling at the beguiling manner in which it wisped about her face. Somehow it seemed as if she had more hair rather than less. Channing frowned now because he was going to have to eat some crow.

Simon put away the hair-dryer, squirted some goop into his palm and worked it haphazardly into Jolie's hair, tugging here, smoothing there, until he achieved the look he wanted.

Then he whipped out a hand-held mirror, whirled the chair and brought both hands to his lean hips. "Well?"

Jolie studied the back of her head, fingering the curling wisps of vibrant hair at her nape. Suddenly, Channing's palms itched to fill themselves with that hair, to smooth and tug and sweep. Simon turned to him then, pivoting on his toes.

"Well?"

Channing didn't take his eyes off Jolie as he said, "She's beautiful."

"Of *course,* she's *beautiful,*" Simon scoffed. "What *do* you *think* of her *hair?*"

Channing licked his lips and forced out the words. "Her hair looks great."

Jolie laughed. Simon crowed, clapping his hands together. Turning back to Jolie, he advised, "Make *him* take *you* out and *show* you *off,* girlfriend."

Jolie settled her smile on Channing. "We'll see."

The last thing he wanted to do was show her off. He'd much rather have locked her away in a big room with a bed and an endless supply of candlelight and wine. Something in his gaze must have said so, because Jolie blushed and turned away.

Chico started up his dryer then, and Channing reluctantly turned his attention to his daughter, who was squinting without her glasses. Chico spoke all the while he was drawing her hair out with a round brush and applying hot air to it.

"You can just let it air-dry, but brush it under while it's still damp, and you'll need a trim every six to eight weeks. When you get a little older, honey, we'll put some highlights in. Oh, my stars, aren't you adorable? I'll show you some easy ways to fix it, kind of change it up." He went on and on, drying her hair strand by strand.

Channing was unaware of having risen until he felt Jolie's

hand on his wrist and looked down to find her standing next to him. He glanced at her face and then turned back to his daughter. The hair that curved under just above her shoulders was shining and healthy, thick and full. In contrast, her face seemed a little thinner, her brows, which were a shade darker than her hair, a little fuller. He had never noticed her brows before, the graceful way they arched and swept. He had never noticed her mouth either, the pretty, bow shape of it. Chico fooled around several minutes longer after he put aside the dryer, sweeping hair this way and that, talking non-stop. Finally, he handed Phil her glasses.

Phil carefully slid them on her face, sitting forward slightly in the chair. Channing watched her eyes as they grew large behind the lenses, then larger still.

"Oh!"

"Glorious hair," Chico pronounced. "Mm-mm-mm."

Phil shoved her hands into the swinging mass and watched it thread through her fingers like silk.

"Oh!"

"You'll be able to do lots more with it," Chico said. "And here, let me show you something else." He opened a drawer beneath the mirror and rummaged around, producing several pairs of glasses frames. Producing a large, hand-held mirror, he had Phil try on the smaller frames, showing her how fashionable she could look. The wonder and eagerness on her face tore at Channing's heart.

"Can I, Chan?" she asked breathlessly. "Can I?"

As if a new pair of glasses was a big thing. Emotion swelled up inside of him, and he groped blindly for Jolie's hand, knowing that she was to credit. "Sure, baby," he managed.

"Do you like it?" Phil demanded of him, even as she shoved her old glasses onto her face and swung her head so that her hair swayed about her shoulders.

He nodded, his nose burning with something that felt suspiciously like tears. His hand tightened convulsively around Jolie's. "Very much."

Jolie laughed and Chico made humming sounds that spoke to Channing's ears as, "I told you so." He didn't care. Grinning ear to ear, he hauled out his wallet.

"How much do I owe you?"

Two hundred dollars would have kept his hair cut for a year, but he forked over the amount without a second thought and added a generous tip to it. Then he turned to Simon.

"Oh, no," Jolie said, but Simon was already taking money from his hand—less, thankfully, than his partner had. Maybe they charged by the inch. Jolie was still protesting, but Channing couldn't hear her through his smile. Phil skipped, literally skipped, ahead of them, leading the way down the bright yellow hall and out into the green foyer. She was already on the sidewalk when Channing surprised himself by giving in to sudden impulse. As they reached the door, he hauled Jolie against him, caught her at the nape with his other hand and drove his mouth against hers.

Her hand came up to clutch his wrist, but she didn't pull away. Indeed, her mouth softened beneath his. He wrapped an arm around her and drank of her. He forgot where he was, forgot everything except how good it felt to be this close to her. It hit him in a rush then, how much he'd missed her these past few weeks as she'd devoted her time to Phil instead of him. He had tagged along today, he realized, not to talk them out of this, but merely to spend some time in her company, to find a moment for this. He ached with unfulfilled need, and it frightened him in some way that he couldn't quite put his finger on. Simon brought him back to the present.

"Oo-*eee*. Do *I* do *good* work or *what?*"

Breaking the kiss, Channing turned a scowl over his shoulder and looked over the top of glasses he had forgotten to wear. Simon and Chico grinned at him from the doorway, the beaded curtain pushed aside to frame their tall and small frames. Channing grimaced and looked to the desk, where the bobbing head gaped at him openly. Sighing, he pushed Jolie through the door and onto the sidewalk, heat blasting them. It was then that Jolie chortled, and suddenly everything else drained away. Channing felt himself smiling, and then laughter fountained up. Phil was standing with both hands on her hips, looking at them both as if they'd lost their minds.

"What?"

Channing shook his head. "That glasses place," he said, feeling light as air, "the one that makes them up in an hour, don't they have one in the mall?"

Phil was crossing the street before he caught her admonition to hurry. Jolie started after her. Channing stepped off with quick strides to snag Jolie's hand, folding it into his own as they followed. Life was suddenly good. Very, very good. And puzzling. Unsettling in a way that he didn't want to study. But then, why should he? Everything was going his way. Jolie was growing closer and closer to capitulation, whether she realized it or not, and Phil was slowly getting used to the idea of having her around permanently. More to the point, Jolie was every bit as good for Phil as he had known she would be. Just witness that happy-go-lucky kid who couldn't wait to get to the mall and show off her new hairstyle. He had nothing to worry about, nothing at all. So what was missing? What was it that lifted the hair on the nape of his neck from time to time and made him want to bury his head under the ever-growing pile of papers in his office? Whatever it was, he shook it off, not daring to look too closely.

* * *

He was doing it. Somehow, despite everything, Chan was winning. And now that he was, she sensed that he regretted it, at least in some part of himself. Jolie stared at the band shell where an orchestra in shirtsleeves played a spectacular selection of Mozart, and felt Channing with every fiber of her being. He sat next to her on the blanket, his bare knees drawn up, one arm draped across them while his other hand lightly covered her ankle. She had removed her sandals and spread out her full blue skirt before arranging herself on the blanket, her feet angled to one side. Channing had taken the spot next to her, opened the small cooler he had carried into the park and poured a glass of iced sangria for each of them and Benny and Dessie, who shared the blanket behind them with Phil and Mona.

As darkness had settled and the orchestra had gathered for tuning, the greensward had begun to fill up with other concert-goers, their spirits buoyed by a steady, cooling breeze. Phil had chased Mona around the two blankets spread on the grass until Mona had collapsed in a heap and settled in for a nap. Phil lay next to her now, staring at that chubby face endlessly as if trying to see something hidden there, perhaps a sense of herself as a toddler, before her great difference from the rest of the human race had made itself known.

Citronella torches ringed the perimeter of the concert area and marked off proper aisles in the open expanse, casting an amber glow over the faces of the listeners. Manicured inches of thick, irrigated lawn cushioned their blankets, and special outdoor speakers mounted in trees and on poles guaranteed the quality of the sound, while night kept the city and all its bustle at bay. Jolie felt cocooned in a languid sea of glorious sound and gentle sensation, where her personal will ebbed into quiescence.

Why shouldn't she give in? She was in love with him. Every time he touched her with that casual, proprietary affection that seemed to come so easily to him, she felt that love kick and stretch her heart. Like a child growing in her belly, it tumbled and poked and kept itself known, a living entity both separate from her and an inseparable part of her. As the music crescendoed, Channing's hand slid up beneath the hem of her dress, lightly massaging the calf of one leg. Jolie closed her eyes, awash with feeling.

Almost two-thirds of her time was gone. Nearly two months had vanished like a wisp of smoke in a stiff breeze. Channing had not mentioned marriage in weeks, and though he regularly curled her toes with his deep, hot kisses, he had said no more about altering their agreement, either. More and more lately he left her on her own with Phil, who showed signs of warming up, especially if Mona was to be around, and Channing made sure that Mona and Dessie and Ben were around a good deal. She was confused about that.

Perhaps he simply meant to be kind. Perhaps he enjoyed the company of her friends as much as she did. Perhaps he was just indulging Phil. But it felt like something more, something she couldn't quite put her finger on, and it troubled her. A great deal troubled her. Jolie wanted to believe that a marriage between them would work, despite all the odds. She wanted to believe it with a desperation that frightened and disoriented her. In some ways, she didn't know herself anymore. She had meant to help Phil, despite the girl's antipathy, but somehow it had all become about Channing. And herself.

The infrequent nights that she spent at his house had become torturous exercises in waiting and hoping and wondering and fearing. Every time, she expected a tap at her door, a heartfelt rush of pleas, a surge of passionate persuasion. She never quite decided if she would give in or not, but she definitely wanted the experience. Yet, his kisses were public now, never private except with the constant expectation of discovery. It was as if he beckoned and tempted with one hand and held her off with the other, and she never knew what to do about it. How did she let him know that she wanted more without betraying her feelings and opening herself up to…what? Pain? Rejection? Both? Yes, both, despite the fact that he was persuading her to marry him.

Had she really thought at one time that marriage without love might be the only safe option? Or had she always known that no such safety existed for her? She didn't know anymore. She just didn't know.

The orchestra played a final number, bringing those not snoozing on the grass to their feet. The applause sounded muted and insufficient after the captivating intricacy of the music. Jolie sighed, unwilling to let the melody go, the night end, but Channing was packing the cooler while Dessie picked up stray bits of litter and stuffed them into a plastic bag. Benny went down on one knee to gather up an oblivious Mona, who lolled like an overstuffed rag doll in his arms, and Jolie began helping Phil fold up the blankets. All too quickly, the party was packed up and ready to go. Following the rest of the crowd, they filed out into the grass corridor and inched toward the exit. Channing carried the cooler with one hand and rested the other upon Jolie's shoulder, but the moment they reached the parking lot, he moved away from her. She missed the contact, and she knew that it wouldn't come again this evening—unless she somehow found the courage to take the initiative.

Ben and Dessie belted a rousing Mona into her car seat in the back of Benny's small station wagon, then said their good-byes and drove away as Chan stowed the cooler and Phil climbed into the narrow back seat of the truck. Phil was talking about how she could never play music like those in the orchestra, then began telling Jolie about her latest drama class. Chan said nothing as he climbed beneath the wheel and started the engine. While they were moving at a snail's pace toward the street, Phil decided that she needed a snow cone. She pleaded with Chan to hurry to the stand before it closed.

He slid a look at Jolie. "Do you mind?"

She shook her head. Phil sat back, and they drove in silence through the city streets.

A long line of cars was waiting at the drive-thru of the small snow cone stand, so Chan pulled over, and Jolie got out to let Phil exit the truck in order to stand in line at the window. Channing rolled down the windows and killed the engine. As Jolie climbed back into her seat, she knew that she wasn't likely to get a better moment to broach the subject on her mind.

"You've been quiet lately."

He looked over at her in some surprise. "Have I?"

She reached across the console. "Is something wrong, Chan?"

He stroked a hand through his hair bemusedly. "Why ever would you think that?"

"I don't know. You've been...distant."

"Sorry. I didn't realize. I guess I'm preoccupied with work. The closer we come to launch, the more problems we have, it seems. The last shipment of hologram labels was almost indistinguishable. We're wrangling with the supplier now, and I can't help wondering if we wouldn't be better off making the darn things ourselves."

Jolie looked away, disappointed that he had chosen to turn the conversation away from the personal. "Have you spoken to Benny about it?" she mumbled dutifully.

"As a matter of fact, I have." He went on, recounting the discussion, until Jolie thought she would scream.

Suddenly she heard herself demanding, "Why are you doing this?"

Channing stared at her, something oddly vulnerable in his eyes. Then he cleared his throat and glanced away. "I'm sorry. I offended you. I thought you wanted to talk."

"I do, but not about business."

"Okay. Fine. What exactly do you want to talk about?"

"I want to know what's going on with you," she insisted, but he shook his head and chuckled.

"What do you want me to say? I just told you."

"Don't patronize me," she snapped angrily, as surprised at herself as he was. He leaned toward her, apology written on his face. "Have you changed your mind?" she blurted.

"About what?"

"Wanting to marry me."

"No! Have you?"

She should say yes. She could say it, and the rest wouldn't matter. He would marry her. They'd hammer out an iron-clad pre-nup, a contract to end all contracts, and her future would be secured. Except, that wouldn't be enough. She'd sensed it before; she knew it now. She couldn't marry without love. Once, she'd thought that meant that she couldn't marry at all. Now she knew the truth about herself, and it was exactly as she'd always feared. She wanted, needed, that most dangerous of all emotional entanglements. She wanted Channing to love her. But, of course, he couldn't. He wanted her, yes, but love her?

She shook her head. He sat back with a gusted sigh, and for a moment she expected argument, protest, but he said nothing. Nothing. And she realized then that he wasn't winning at all. Neither of them were. Neither of them could. Not like this.

"Tell me about your first marriage," she said carefully.

He shrugged and glanced out his window. "Nothing to tell that I haven't already told you."

"How did you meet?"

He licked his lips. "At work."

She asked the one question for which she really had to have an answer. "Did you love her?"

He straightened agitatedly, and for a moment she thought that he was going to ignore the question, but then he said softly, "I don't know." He took a deep breath and went on. "I thought I did, but after a couple of years, I realized that it was never going to be what I had expected. Then suddenly Phil was mine, and I knew I didn't, couldn't, feel a fraction of what I felt for her for Amanda. There was an odd relief when Amanda left. I missed having someone with me, another adult. I missed the sex, frankly. But I've never honestly missed Amanda herself. And obviously she's never missed me. We haven't spoken since the day we signed the divorce papers."

Jolie sighed, as troubled as relieved. She couldn't help remembering that Phil had claimed he was still in love with his ex. Now she almost wished that were true. "Why me, Chan?" she had to ask.

He looked at her then, as clearly puzzled as she was herself. "I don't know how to answer that exactly. I've been operating via my instincts for a long time now. I didn't have any other choice after Phil came to me. I was so completely out of my depth with her that I couldn't do anything else, and in all honesty, I don't think I've done half bad, not with Phil and not with the business. So when you barged into my office that day and everything in me started screaming, 'That's her. That's the one you've been looking for,' I just naturally listened. I knew I had to get you with Phil, be sure you were right for her."

"But what about *you,* Chan?" Jolie asked, both desperate and afraid to hear the answer. "Am I right for *you?*"

He opened his mouth, then closed it again, ran a hand over his face. "I don't know what you want me to say."

"I want you to answer my question. Am I right for you?"

He seemed to have as much difficulty saying the words as she did hearing them. "I feel as if I know you on some level I can't quite pinpoint. I think we pretty much want the same things, see life the same way. I trust you, respect you. I'm very much looking forward to having you with us permanently." He reached for her hand, clutched it almost painfully and added softly, silkily, "I can't wait to have you in my bed."

But can you love me? her heart screamed. It was the most important question, the one answer she simply had to know, but even as she opened her mouth to ask it, the door at her side swung away.

"Half piña colada, half blueberry," Phil announced happily, waving a large snow cone beneath Jolie's nose. "Took long enough," she added, lipping up a bite of the syrup-flavored shaved ice.

Swallowing her disappointment with no small measure of perverse relief, Jolie opened the third door and scooted her seat forward so Phil could climb into the back seat. Phil slammed the door and locked it. Jolie closed her own and smiled lamely at Chan as he started the engine and rolled up the windows. She thought about asking Chan not to drop her off yet, to take her home with him so they could talk after Phil had gone to bed, but she couldn't do it. She had skated as close to the truth as she dared for one evening, and she knew that it would be some time before she could work up her courage to do it again. So she said nothing as Chan guided the big truck through the busy city to her own apartment. She could have broached the subject once more as he walked her to her door, but instead she merely turned her face up for his good-night kiss and tried to tell herself that it didn't matter. She wouldn't marry him. She couldn't. No matter how much she wanted to.

Chapter Nine

Phil answered the door that next Saturday afternoon. "Hey. I didn't know you were coming."

It was a far cry from a warm welcome, but also a long way from the vitriol with which Jolie had been greeted early on. "Did I misunderstand? Didn't your father say to come for lunch?"

Phil shrugged impatiently. "I don't know." At the sound of footsteps in the stairwell behind her, she whirled away, saying, "You came down." Quickly, she began making gestures with her hands. "Come and meet Jolie."

Curiosity piqued, Jolie edged forward, peering into the stairwell. A girl just a few inches taller than Phil, with a cap of sleek, dark hair, eased down the last step and out into the foyer, her large brown eyes alive with shy intelligence.

"This is Jolie," Phil said, gesturing with her hands. Jolie realized with a shock that Phil was spelling out her name in sign language. Phil smiled at Jolie, saying, "This is my friend, Sadie.'' She interpreted her own words with sign language, adding, ''She's deaf.''

''I assumed as much,'' Jolie said, and waited for Phil to interpret. She stretched out her hand. ''Hello, Sadie. It's nice to meet you.''

Sadie briefly touched her hand, then signed a reply, which Phil interpreted. ''Nice to meet you, too. You don't look like a wooden Indian.''

Jolie smiled. Obviously Phil had mentioned her. ''Thank you.''

''Chan's in the den,'' Phil said, still signing so Sadie wouldn't feel left out of the conversation. ''Sadie's helping me with something. See ya.'' With that both girls turned and ran up the stairs, leaving Jolie to stare after them, a warm feeling creeping over her. Phil had a friend, a real friend her own age. Grinning broadly, Jolie turned and sauntered down the entry hall to the den.

Chan started when she walked into the room, swiveling around in his chair. ''Oh, hi.'' He got to his feet. ''Is it that time already?''

Deflated, Jolie glanced around her. No television. No music. No book or magazine or paper. ''You said eleven-thirty.''

''Oh, right. Sure. I just...lost track, I guess. Did Phil let you in?''

Jolie nodded affirmatively. ''I met her friend.''

''Sadie,'' Channing said, smiling. ''She's deaf.''

''Yes, I know. When did this happen?''

''Not long ago. Phil was serving as a theatre usher at a matinee for the hearing-impaired. It's part of the class requirements. Anyway, Sadie was there with a group. Somehow they got to talking—well, not talking exactly. Anyway, Phil came right home and taught herself sign language. Then the next time they had a performance for the hearing-impaired, Sadie was there again with her mother, and Phil formally introduced herself."

Jolie chuckled. "Taught herself sign language," she mused, shaking her head. "That's our Phil."

Channing rocked back on his heels, smiling with satisfaction. "Sadie's eleven, a little shy, but intelligent and quite mature. Her mother seems delighted with the friendship."

"I'm glad," Jolie said. "I'm really glad."

"Me, too."

He stood there staring at her, seeming at a loss for words. An awkwardness that had never before been present seemed to envelop them. It was as if an elephant had wandered into the room and they were both determined to ignore it. Jolie wished desperately that she hadn't come, that she didn't feel this *discomfort.* Cravenly, she decided on a blatant lie.

"Uh, listen, I can't stay. I, um, forgot that I'd...promised Dessie that I'd...take her and Mona shopping." She went on lamely, muttering, "It's a two-person job, shopping with a kid."

She saw from the look in his eyes that he didn't believe her but was willing to let the lie stand. He didn't want her there any more than she wanted to be there at that moment, and for some reason that hurt more than she could have expected.

"You, um, you should've just called," he said, lifting an arm to indicate that he'd walk her out. She turned into the foyer almost blindly.

"Oh, but that way I'd have missed meeting Sadie."

A smile quirked at the corners of his mouth. "True."

They walked side-by-side through the foyer to the front door without saying another word. Once there, Channing turned her to face him. His fingertips skimmed her cheek and jaw. For a moment, she thought that he meant to kiss her, but then he stepped back, offered her a limp smile and said, "I'll call you later."

It took every ounce of her willpower to merely nod and walk out. What would have happened if she'd given in to the impulse to grab him by the shirt front and demand answers to the questions tormenting her? Or perhaps she had her answers and simply couldn't let herself acknowledge them. She didn't know why it even mattered since she had no intention whatsoever of marrying the man, because one thing she did know absolutely was that the most finely drawn, iron-clad contract in the world could not protect the heart.

Channing closed the door at Jolie's back. What was wrong with him? He didn't want her to go, but he couldn't quite bear for her to stay, either. This made no sense, no sense at all. When they were apart, he couldn't quite seem to think of anything else. Even when he was working, she was never very far from his mind. Then, in unguarded moments, he would feel a sudden need to see her, to assure himself that she was available and amenable, a need so strong that it shook him, almost frightened him. No, that couldn't be right. What was there to fear? If—*when*—they married, it would be a sensible, firmly negotiated, unbreakable contract, leaving nothing to chance, a very comfortable, thoughtful arrangement which would address the needs and expectations of both. Life would go on much as it did now, with the obvious exception of a great deal of improvement in his sex life—and hers, as well, of course. What more could a man want? God knew she'd proven good as gold for Phil, just as he'd hoped.

This anxiety, this *neediness,* would no doubt disappear once the contract was inked and the wedding performed.

So why then did this shivery feeling so often creep up

his spine to lift the fine hairs on the back of his neck? Why did his chest literally ache sometimes? Why did he lie awake at night, staring at the phone on his bedside table and telling himself that it was foolish and pointless to call her up just to hear the sound of her voice? He stood there, his hands curled into fists that would not relax until he heard her drive away, and then, once she was well and truly gone, the house seemed suddenly empty and bereft, which made no sense at all because Phil had a friend, a real friend, right up those stairs there.

He tried to think what he'd do with himself now that his lunch plans were broken; then he wondered what he'd done with himself since Sadie had arrived, and he knew with true self-disgust that they were likely to be one and the same thing. He was going to mope and wonder and skirt around the edges of what he seemed unable to intelligently consider, avoiding Jolie even as he craved her company. It seemed to him that the only solution to his dilemma was to put an end to this ridiculous courtship phase and simply marry the woman. That way life could settle into some semblance of normalcy, these contrary feelings would disappear, and he could return to being his old self again. Unfortunately, he didn't think he could convince Jolie to go along with this alteration in their agreement.

Massaging his temples where a dull headache had started, he went to make lunch for Phil and her little friend, a long, boring afternoon stretching out before him.

Now at loose ends, Jolie couldn't quite decide what to do with herself. Maybe if she went to see Dessie, as she'd told Chan she was going to, she could talk out the confusion plaguing her. With that goal in mind, she eventually drove to Dessie's small frame house. The fifties-era, two-bedroom home sorely needed painting. The peeling white of the wood siding and faded pink of the shutters depressed Jolie as she swung her car into the rough, buckled drive. The cement steps had finally come loose from the narrow, crumbling porch, leaving a dangerous three-inch gap at the top. Surely Dessie would fix up the place now that they had a genuine income. Jolie made a mental note to mention it later. Right now she had other things on her mind.

Exiting the car, she gingerly made her way to the house, up the stairs and across the porch to the front door. She knocked and then impatiently knocked twice more before Mona's wail confirmed that Dessie was, indeed, at home. It was still some moments before Dessie opened the door, but the instant she did, Jolie pushed past her, having had enough of the melting heat and her friend's slothful response to her summons. Once inside, she shoved her sunshades up onto the top of her head and found herself blinded by the relative dark indoors.

"Jo!" Dessie exclaimed. "I wasn't expecting you."

"Just don't tell Chan that," Jolie admonished, slinging her purse into a chair and following it down to drop her head into her hands. "The man is driving me nuts!"

Mona wailed in the next room. "In a minute, baby," Dessie called.

"I don't know what to do," Jolie went on. "I can't figure out what's going on. Help me make sense of this!"

Dessie was still standing in the middle of the room. "Um, listen, let me get dressed right quick and—"

"Dressed?" Jolie echoed, looking up, her eyes having adjusted enough to reveal Dessie standing before her in nothing more than a towel, her hair streaming wetly down her back. "Oh, gosh, I got you out of the shower. I'm sorry."

"It's all right," Dessie said, moving away. "Just give me a minute to—"

Suddenly another figure appeared in the doorway between the small living room and the dining room, backlighted by the sunshine streaming through the uncovered kitchen windows beyond. "Honey, did you see this rash on Mona? No wonder she keeps stripping off her diaper. We have any—" He broke off, staring at Jolie, who was staring at him. His dark hair and the tank he wore with soft, knit shorts were wet. Just like Dessie. "Oops. Uh, hi, Jo."

She didn't want to believe it, but the endearment with which he'd addressed Dessie was still ringing in her ears, just as another word clanged in her mind. *Duped.* Duped by her two best friends. Suddenly she was remembering other times over the past weeks and months when she'd sensed that something was different. How many times had she got the impression that she'd interrupted or missed something important? Jolie got to her feet, saying tightly, "Benny."

"We, uh…that is, *I* was, ah…"

"Taking a shower?" Jolie provided sharply. She scraped her gaze over Dessie, letting them both know that, stupid as she obviously was, she hadn't been born yesterday.

"We were going to tell you," Dessie said resignedly. "We just… It never seemed like the right time."

But Jolie was glaring at Benny, who now regarded her calmly, his arms folded across his chest. "How could you?" she asked, feeling wild inside, abandoned. She could think of only one explanation. "You knew she was vulnerable after John left. You were her friend and partner, not to mention mine. How could you take advantage of her like this?"

"That's enough," Dessie said quietly, but it couldn't be. Jolie couldn't let it be.

"He was our friend," she insisted, "our partner. He took advantage! He—"

"No!" Dessie interrupted, tugging her towel more tightly around her and snugging the end beneath one arm. "You're not going to blame Benny for this. He wanted to tell you all along. I'm the one who wanted it kept quiet. I knew you wouldn't, couldn't, understand."

"Understand?" Jolie snapped. "What's to understand? You were vulnerable after John. He took advantage."

"I love Benny!" Dessie exclaimed, and to Jolie it was the death knell of something else, a relationship she had depended upon since college, the one sure thing in a constantly changing world. Desperately, she grasped at straws.

"W-we both love him, b-but you w-were the v-vulnerable one, and he took advantage of that."

"We're getting married, Jo," Dessie said. "Soon now."

Jolie literally reeled. She looked to Benny. "You've ruined it," she accused hollowly. "It's always been the three of us, the Three Musketeers. Best friends. Partners! And now you've ruined it!"

"Jolie, please," he said miserably, "you know I love you like a sister, always have."

"And Dessie," she shot back. "Do you love her like a sister, too?"

"No," he said gently.

"What changed it, Benny?" she demanded angrily. "John leaving? Dessie being in too much pain to think straight?"

"Nothing changed my feelings for Dessie," Benny admitted, "not my marriage, not hers." He shoved a hand over his head, admitting, "Hell, I've been in love with her since college."

"But I only wanted to be friends back then," Dessie added hastily.

"And I took her at her word," Benny said. "If she wanted a friend, a friend is what I'd be. I kept trying to...find someone else. But it's always been Dessie in my heart. When John left, it killed me to see her so hurt."

"And I'd been secretly regretting the friends-only thing for some time," Dessie put in. "I just didn't think I could do anything about it. When I met John, Benny was already married, so I figured, why not?"

"Then everything fell apart," Benny went on, "for both of us, and suddenly we had this second chance."

"But neither of us wanted to hurt you," Dessie said, "and we knew you'd feel betrayed, so we kept it quiet."

"And then Hawkins came along," Benny offered, "and we thought maybe if you were settled with him..."

Jolie's head was spinning. Betrayed. Yes, that was exactly how she felt. Her two best friends were a couple now. *A couple.* And she was out in the cold. As always. It wasn't fair. Suddenly what Benny had implied made itself understood, somewhat belatedly, and Jolie seized on it, poured her anger and fear and pain into it.

"That's why you pushed me at Channing! You were hoping I'd marry him and leave the two of you to...to..." She waved a hand, unable to say it. She thought it, though, and her chin wobbled, the tears that had filled her eyes now spilling over onto her cheeks. Jealousy seared her, not only because they had dared to find that for which she was too fearful to look, but because they had actually found it *together.* Some small part of her knew that it was petty to feel this way, but a larger part, a wounded, needy part, just couldn't control the emotions that tumbled and roiled inside her. "Well, don't come to me when this all blows up in your faces! And don't think I'm going to let myself in for the same thing just to ease your consciences, because I won't! So just go ahead and...d-do whatever, b-but leave me out of it! Just leave me out of it!" With that she grabbed up her purse and stumbled for the door, even as Dessie and Ben both called for her to stay.

Dimly, she heard Mona bawling in the background and

Dessie continuing to call out to her while Benny quietly admonished Dessie to put on some clothes. Somehow she got out the door and down the steps, the sunshine and the tears combining to blind her, then she was running across the lawn and smack into her own car. The chrome door handle was hot from the unrelenting sun, but she barely registered the burn in her palm. She slung her purse inside, followed, then slammed the door and locked it. She clawed her sunshades down onto her face, clearing the worst of the blindness. When she looked up, Benny was standing on the porch, hands on his hips. He watched as she scrambled for her keys, stabbed one into the ignition and started the car. He was still watching as she drove away, Dessie careening into him as she pulled a T-shirt down over the shorts she'd thrown on. He wrapped an arm around Dessie's shoulders, steadying and comforting her as she pushed wet hair off her face, and Jolie began to sob, only one thought in her bursting head. She had lost them. She had lost them all.

Chan was surprised to find Dessie, Ben and Mona at his door on Sunday afternoon.

"Have you spoken to Jolie?" Dessie demanded worriedly.

"Today, you mean?"

"Or yesterday."

"Yesterday morning," he confirmed, "about eleven-thirty. I've tried to call a couple times since but keep getting her machine." The looks on their faces sent his heart plummeting toward his toes. "Why? Has something happened?"

"Can we come in?" Benny suddenly asked, Mona perched on his folded arm. "This is going to take some explaining."

Shaking his head at his own thoughtlessness, Channing hopped out of the way. "Of course. Sure. Come on in. It's hot out there." They walked through the door and stood as he closed it. "Come on back and have a seat," Channing offered, waving them down the hall as he led the way, remembering his manners. "Can I get you something cool to drink?"

"No, thanks," Dessie murmured. "I don't even know if you can help us, really. I'm just so worried about her."

Channing showed them into the den, impatient now to the point of rudeness. "I think you'd better tell me what's happened. Is Jolie hurt?"

"No, not physically," Benny assured him. Then he sighed. "She caught us."

That told Channing absolutely nothing. He brought his hands to his hips, frankly tired of the nonsense. "Caught you?"

Dessie slid an embarrassed look at Benny, cleared her throat and said softly, "We've been having an affair."

Channing's eyebrows went straight into his hairline. He let out a low whistle, weighing the ramifications. "And she *caught* you?"

"Just out of the shower," Dessie said, bitter regret lacing her voice.

Channing lifted a hand to the back of his neck, imagining Jo's reaction to finding that her two best friends were having an affair. Without doubt, it hadn't gone over well. Mona suddenly reached out and snagged a handful of her mother's hair, demanding attention. Channing put aside trying to figure the ramifications and made a decision. "Why don't I ask Phil to take Mona up to the playroom so we can sit down and talk? I have the feeling you'd better tell me everything from the start."

Dessie and Ben agreed, and he went to call Phil, who he knew would be delighted to entertain Mona for a few minutes. Half an hour later, he had a detailed picture of the situation and a fairly good idea of what Jolie must be feeling. Moreover, he knew what he was going to do about it.

"I'm glad you came to me," he told the pair seated before him. "I'll take care of this."

"It may not be that easy," Ben warned him. "Jolie has more reason than most to be wary of love. That's why we were hesitant to let her know what was happening between us, even after we agreed that we would marry."

"Truly?" Channing asked, even as Benny took Dessie's hand in his. "Well, congratulations then. I'm sure Jolie will come around in time for the wedding."

Dessie shook her head. "I don't think so. Besides, we've both done the formal wedding thing, and we want to keep it small and personal this time."

"And we want to do it soon," Benny added. Dessie grimaced, but he insisted. "She knows now, so waiting serves no purpose."

Dessie sighed. "I suppose you're right, but I can't help wishing things were different. She's our dearest friend."

"Even if she doesn't believe so just now," Benny agreed, nodding.

"I know what she's feeling," Dessie said to Channing almost pleadingly. "Her parents were never there for her, so we've always tried to be, and now she feels we've abandoned her, too. She's feeling alone, Chan, and betrayed."

"She won't even talk to us," Benny said.

"She'll talk to me," Channing said flatly. He wouldn't give her any choice, and when he was through, she would know that she need never be alone again. "You two make your plans," he told them, "and let me worry about Jolie." He stood up, anxious to be setting plans of his own into motion and offered them each a hand, saying, "And if there's anything else I can do, you just let me know."

"We'll do that," Benny said.

"I just hope you can get through to her," Dessie added. Chan merely smiled, his mind whirling.

She didn't answer the phone or her door for the remainder of that Sunday, and she didn't go in to the office on Monday, either. Instead, she brooded. Why hadn't she realized what was happening? All those times she'd sensed that something was different, why didn't it occur to her what it was? Yes, she'd been caught up first in starting the agency, then in getting the Hawk contract and then in Channing and Phil, but she should have known. She should have done something, said something to save them all from this...this...disaster in the making, for she was desperately sure that no marriage between Benny and Dessie could last. Not that it mattered now. The old trio was busted, and even after Ben and Dessie's *involvement* was finished, nothing could ever put it back together again, not the way it had been. Bitter and repeated experience had taught her that.

Nevertheless, when her doorbell rang that Monday morning, she couldn't resist just taking a peek out the peep hole to see who was there. Her heart did a glad flip—which she ruthlessly repressed the very next instant—when she saw Channing Hawkins cooling his heels on the walkway.

"I know you're there, Jo. Let me in."

Rebelliously, she started to turn away, but then she really didn't want to and she wasn't foolish enough to cut off her own nose to spite her face. She'd go mad if she stayed in this apartment sulking alone. She turned back and opened the door.

He smiled sympathetically. "Ready to talk?"

"About?"

"Dessie and Ben for starters."

She wrapped her arms around herself. "They told you?"

He nodded and stepped through the door into her tiny

entry alcove. She walked into the living room and left him to close the door himself, which he did before following. She sat in the small wing chair that matched the floral, French country sofa on the opposite wall. Rather than take a seat on that sofa, Channing walked to the sturdy coffee table before it and carefully sat down on its edge, close to Jolie.

"How're you doing?" he asked softly.

She hunched a shoulder. "Okay." Blatant lie number one.

"Everyone's worried about you, especially Dessie and Ben."

She huffed at that. "I'll bet."

"I told them that you're made of sterner stuff than they've given you credit for," he said. "Sure, you're reeling. It had to be a shock, but now that you know, you'll get a handle on it."

"What I don't understand is why they didn't tell me from the beginning." Blatant lie number two. "That's what really gets me. If they'd just been honest—"

"You'd have done everything in your power to derail any romance," he said flatly. "Don't deny it."

"Why should I?" she retorted hotly. "I suppose you would let your two best friends just walk off the side of a cliff without trying to stop them?"

"Is that really what you equate marriage with, walking off the side of a cliff? Because they are getting married—in two weeks, on Saturday."

"I'll send a gift," she snapped.

He lifted a hand to her cheek. "Don't be bitter, Jolie," he said tenderly. "I'm sorry you're hurt, and I know you're feeling alone right now, but you're not."

Tears gathered in her eyes. She blinked them away, whispering, "I've always been alone."

"But you don't have to be," he went on. "You don't have to ever be alone again, not even one more day if that's what you want."

"It's not that simple," she murmured, lost in her own world of disappointment.

"But it is," Channing said, straightening one leg and leaning back slightly to shove a hand into his pants pocket. When he leaned forward again, a diamond ring lay in the palm of his hand, an outlandishly large diamond ring. Jolie's mouth fell open.

"That isn't what I think it is." Hadn't he heard anything she'd just said? Didn't he understand even now that marriage was not a solution for her? For them? No matter how much she wanted it to be.

"You wouldn't be walking off a cliff," he said. "We can negotiate an air-tight contract, hammer down every detail. You'll know exactly what you're getting into. I don't think I need to point out all the advantages at this point. Suffice it to say that we'll both benefit greatly—and you'll never be alone again. I swear it. Just say the word. We can be on our way to Vegas before dark."

Jolie could only stare. "Are you out of your mind?"

"No, of course not," he replied patiently. "If you want a formal wedding, I'm sure we can quickly—"

"A formal wedding?" she echoed. "You are insane."

"Jolie, I'm just offering to—"

"Save me from my disappointment?" she interrupted snidely. "Ride in like a knight on his charger to the rescue, sweep me off my feet?"

A look of consternation flitted across his face before he carefully arranged it once more. "I just thought—"

"That you could take advantage of the situation, turn it to your benefit? You're assuming, of course, that I intend to marry you at all!"

"Come on, Jolie," he said, his tone cajoling. "We both know you're not indifferent to the idea anymore."

"Indifferent?" She laughed harshly. "I'll tell you what I'm not indifferent to. I'm not indifferent to being railroaded, to being taken advantage of. You think that just because Ben and Dessie are stupid enough to f-fall in l-love, that I...that I..." Suddenly afraid that she'd divulged too much, she leapt to her feet and stabbed a finger at the entry. "Get out!"

"Jolie."

"Get out!" When he didn't immediately get to his feet, she grabbed him by the shirt and hauled him up, turning him bodily toward the door. "Get out and stay away."

"Now wait a minute," he began.

"No!" she exclaimed. "It's finished. Do you hear me?" She shoved him, her hands planted firmly between his shoulder blades, and he literally stumbled toward the door. "It's over. Done." She shoved him again, and he finally moved under his own power. She darted around him and yanked open the door. "Go away," she said, "and don't come back."

"Now listen," he said, even as he moved reluctantly through the doorway, "I know you're upset, but we already have a contract in place."

"So sue me!" she shouted, pushing him through the opening. "The courtship is officially over, and thank you, but no thank you, Mr. Hawkins. I'd rather marry an ice cube! At least it would warm up!" With that she slammed the door, her anger so great that it was a good quarter-hour after he finally went away before she began to weep again.

Phil climbed into the pickup and fastened her safety belt. "Enjoy your day with Sadie?"

"Very much. How was your day?"

He shrugged and started the truck moving once more. "So-so."

"You saw Jolie today," she prodded, and Chan sighed, knowing that if he didn't say it he'd burst.

"I asked her to marry me today, and she threw me out of her apartment like I'd insulted her!"

Phil clucked her tongue and shook her head. "Please tell me you didn't bring up that contract nonsense again."

Channing shot her a surprised look, then made a completely unnecessary lane change. "What do you know about that?"

"Everything," she said complacently.

"How—" he began, breaking off when she slid him a mischievous look. "Never mind. I don't want to know."

She giggled. Giggled. His Phil. Suddenly the world didn't look quite so grim. "You did offer her a contract marriage, didn't you?" she pressed.

"Of course, I did. It's the only sensible way to go about it."

"Oh, sure."

He knew sarcasm when he heard it. "People do it all the time," he said defensively, slowing for a stop sign. "You've heard of prenuptial agreements. Well, this is sort of like that, only it would guarantee no divorce, among other things. It's for her protection as much as mine."

"Jolie doesn't need a pre-nup," Phil said gently. "She needs to know you love her."

His foot slipped off the brake pedal, and the truck lurched out into the intersection. Across the way, a sedan's horn blew. Chan shrugged an apology and waved it on across before putting his foot to the gas. "I don't think you understand," he said, once they were through the intersection.

"I understand that you love her," Phil said evenly. "And I understand that she needs to know it."

Chan glanced at her. "How? How do you know?"

She turned a little in her seat, cocking her head to one side. "You know, it was never the idea that you might love Jolie. It was the notion, however stupid, that *she* might not love *me*."

"Oh, Phil, honey," he said. "That was Amanda, not Jolie. Amanda was...Amanda couldn't love anyone, not me, not you, not anyone."

"I know," she said, her voice small and quiet. "But still it hurts, especially when you're different. People stay away from you, and you start to think that everybody hates you. Oh, not you, Chan. I know you love me."

"With all my heart, honey."

"But someone else? Jolie? I was pretty awful right from the beginning," she admitted. "I expected her to hate me. I tried to make her hate me. But she wouldn't, couldn't. Even though she had no reason to, she tried to be my friend, to help me find other friends and a way to like myself."

"You speak as if *you* love her," Channing said softly.

Phil shrugged. "You can't hardly help it, can you?"

He had to laugh. "No, I guess not. Are you saying that you now want me to marry her?"

Phil shrugged. "Hey, when you're right, you're right. Even you, sometimes."

"Gee, thanks."

"So why don't you tell her how you feel?"

Why didn't he? he wondered, but he already knew the answer to that. It was stark terror. What if he spilled his guts and she laughed in his face? On the other hand, she'd already broken it off. What did he have to lose? After a moment he said, "She wouldn't believe it."

"You won't know unless you try."

His fist tightened on the steering wheel. "She won't speak

to me, Phil. I've tried all day. I even sent her flowers with a note, but she refused them."

"Hm," Phil said consideringly. "Maybe you better let me handle this."

"Ha! Famous last words."

"Okay," she said, "let me ask you this." She shifted in her seat again. "Can I keep Mona while Dessie and Ben go off to get married?"

"What? Oh, Phil, I don't know. You're good with Mona, that's a fact, but a weekend can be a long time with a baby. It's just too much for a kid your age. Frankly, I don't think I'm up for it myself."

"No?" she said nonchalantly. "You suppose Jolie is?"

Chan opened his mouth to tell her how preposterous the notion was, but then he thought of all that Jolie had already done for Phil, and he closed it again, thinking hard. After a few moments, he said simply, "Yes." A glance showed him that Phil was grinning ear-to-ear. "Have I ever told you just how glad I am that you're a genius?" he asked, smiling.

Phil tilted her chin smugly. "Since you're in a yes mood, can I ask something else?"

"Sure, baby, go ahead."

"Can I spend the night with Sadie tomorrow?"

A sleepover. A real sleepover. Channing swallowed a lump and said, "You bet."

Phil smiled and turned her face toward her window, suddenly very interested in the passing scenery. Channing looked out the windshield and told God that Jolie had worked this small miracle in their lives, and he couldn't lose her now. He just couldn't.

Chapter Ten

"Please, Jolie, *pleeease.*"

Jolie sat forward, elbows on her desk top, and squeezed her temples with the thumb and little finger of one hand while holding the telephone receiver to her ear with the other. She had somehow managed to live through the most awful ten days of her life. She had gathered her courage, stiffened her backbone, shelved her emotions and walked back into her office, taking up the reins of business with smooth efficiency, but it had been more than merely difficult.

She had made peace with her partners. They did seem happy—guilty perhaps—but happy. For the first time, Jolie saw the love shining in Benny's eyes when he looked at Dessie and Mona. It made her sad in a way, but who was she to deny happiness to her friends, just because she couldn't have it herself? The truth was that she was envious and felt more than a little abandoned, reason enough not to spend a long weekend at the Hawkinses' house. And now

Phil was begging her to help baby-sit Mona so Dessie and Ben could elope.

She cleared her throat. "Look, Phil. I don't think this is a very good idea. Dessie's mom can look after Mona."

"But I want to!" Phil whined. "Please, please. Chan says I'm not old enough to take care of her all on my own."

"Then let Channing—"

"He says he doesn't know enough about little kids her age. Please, Jolie. There's nobody else to ask."

It was tempting, frankly, but she had no business spending a weekend with Channing Hawkins after canceling their "courtship." If only he had developed genuine feelings for her, if he could just see beyond his stupid contract, they might have a chance of... No, she wasn't going to think like that. She'd promised herself, repeatedly, that she wasn't going to play those kinds of wishing games. "Phil, I'm sorry," she began, only to be cut off by a very practiced whine.

"Please, Jo. You said you were my friend. Aren't you? Aren't you my friend anymore?"

"Yes, of course, but—"

"Sadie's mom says she can come to help on Saturday. Sadie just loves babies, and so do I. You won't have to do too much, I promise. Please, Jolie, please, just for me."

Jolie found that she didn't have the strength to keep turning her down. She closed her eyes, certain she was going to regret this, yet, she had no intention of abandoning Phil. Might as well learn to cope with the situation as it was now. Sighing, she capitulated. "Okay. You win. What time Friday morning do Des and Ben want to drop her off?"

Phil whooped. "All right! All right! Thank you, Jo. Thank you, thank you, thank you!"

Jolie couldn't help laughing, even as she prodded, "What time?"

"About ten. Their flight's at eleven-thirty."

"I'll be there."

"Thanks so much, Jolie," Phil said, sobering somewhat. "I mean it. Not just for this, but for everything. You've been a great friend, maybe the first one I ever had."

A lump crowded Jolie's throat. "Oh, Phil."

"I know I was a stinker," Phil went on, "but you liked me anyway, didn't you?"

"Yes, from the very beginning."

"I like you, too, Jo. Really I do." She made a very girlish, very happy sound. "We're gonna have so much fun!"

Jolie had her doubts about that, but she wasn't willing to dampen the child's enthusiasm. "I'll see you Friday."

They hung up giggling. Only later did Jolie's sense of dread overtake her once more. A weekend with Phil and a weekend with Channing were two very different prospects. How on earth was she going to get through one without ruining the other?

Channing had never felt so nervous. He was in over his head, no doubt about it, but what could he do except keep paddling and hope for the best? By the time the doorbell rang at a quarter to ten, he was as nervous as a fish dangling at the end of a line. Still, he managed to stay where he was, pretending interest in a banal morning television talk show. He heard Phil greeting Jolie and knew that the two of them hugged. Warmth burst in his chest, expanded to fill his body and dwindled away to icy terror.

Suddenly he couldn't believe he had agreed to this. What kind of idiot was he to be taking relationship advice from a nine-year-old, even a nine-year-old as intelligent as his daughter? He resisted the urge to bolt and concentrated harder on the television, where some goofy woman was spouting off about technology decimating culture.

"Chan, Jolie's here."

He turned a glance over his shoulder, and his heart dropped. Damn, she looked good enough to eat in slim, cropped white pants and a white lace top worn over some kind of white elastic tube. She'd pinned back part of her bangs with a tiny, frosted butterfly clip, and the effect was absolutely charming. Phil, meanwhile, had used a dozen of the things to pull her thick hair into a bunch of little clumps, which she had then secured at the back of her hair in a single ponytail. She had taken many pains with her hair lately. She and Sadie spent hours at it, sometimes with outlandish effects.

"You look cool," he said to Jolie, meaning it literally. She took it the same way.

"In this weather?" she scoffed. "It's hot enough to melt metal out there."

"Maybe that's why Ben and Dessie chose Niagara Falls," he said, congratulating himself on being able to make conversation.

Jolie said nothing, just glanced around and asked of no one in particular, "Is Mona here yet?"

"Not yet," Phil said lightly. "Want a cold drink?"

"Sure."

They hadn't made it across the hall when the doorbell rang again. Channing got up and followed them to the door. Phil got there first, wrenching open the door enthusiastically. The next several minutes were spent in greetings and getting the necessary paraphernalia into the house and up the stairs to the room next door to Phil's. Then everyone tramped downstairs again.

"Come in and sit down a minute," Channing said, watching Phil heft Mona onto her hip while Mona reached for the butterfly clips atop Phil's head.

"We really don't have time," Ben said.

Dessie reached out one hand to Channing and the other to Jolie. "Thank you both for this. You, too, Phil. It means a lot." She stared at Jolie imploringly. For a moment, Channing thought Jolie would pass up the silent invitation in Dessie's eyes, but she finally leaned forward and looped an arm around the shorter woman's neck. "Don't worry. With Phil around Mona won't even know you're gone."

Dessie threw both arms around Jolie and hugged her tightly, whispering, "Try to understand."

"I will. I do," Jolie said lightly, too much so to be believable. Ben placed his hands on Dessie's shoulders.

"Better go, sweetheart."

Dessie moved to Phil, whom she kissed on the cheek before enveloping both Phil and Mona in a hug and covering Mona's face with kisses. "I'll miss you, baby. Be good."

Mona continued to pluck at the clips in Phil's hair. Ben leaned down and kissed the top of her head, saying simply, "Bye, sugar. Love you."

For him she puckered up for a second kiss and even waved. "Bye-bye, Dada."

"Traitor," Dessie teased, but she was smiling widely, even as she went out the door.

Everything was just ducky until that door closed, at which point Mona suddenly looked around, opened her mouth and screeched like a banshee. Jolie rolled her eyes, muttering, "I knew that was too easy." She took Mona from Phil, who was jiggling her in an attempt to calm her. Mona wrapped her arms around Jolie's neck and screamed for her mama.

"What do we do?" Channing asked worriedly, bitterly disappointed when Jolie sighed and roughly informed him, "Your guess is as good as mine."

In the end, they placated Mona with sugar and constant attention. While the baby sniffed and munched cookies, pausing only occasionally to demand, "Mo," Phil, Jolie and

Chan took turns rescuing everything within her reach. By nightfall, the house was a wreck, the sofa stained, at least two of his videotapes had been hopelessly mangled, and Channing was exhausted. Unfortunately, Mona was still going strong, screaming like a stuck pig every time she didn't get her way and careening around in a constant state of near catastrophe. He was trying to remember why he'd agreed to this stupid plan when Jolie plopped down on the sofa next to him.

"I never should've given her all those cookies," she moaned.

"I never should've caved in to Phil," he muttered.

"That makes two of us," Jolie retorted.

"Why did you?" he asked softly, hoping against hope that she might have had second thoughts about putting an end to their arrangement.

Just then Mona squealed and Phil called out urgently, "Jo! Chan! Come quick!"

They glanced at each other, each looking at the face of panic mixed with resignation. Then they both smiled and, shaking their heads, hauled themselves up and went to see what latest havoc Mona had wrought.

It was well after midnight when Jolie heard the now all-too-familiar wail. She had left all the doors standing open between Mona's room next to Phil's and her own, the same one she'd had every time she'd stayed overnight here, next to Chan's. Somehow she'd never been able to sleep in this lovely French room. No matter how hard she'd tried or how exhausted she'd been, she could never quite shut down when she was here. She could never forget that Channing Hawkins slept right next door. So, she was wide-awake when the first thin wail wafted through the house.

She slipped from the bed in the dark and padded barefoot

in her shortie pajamas out of the room, across the hall, through the exercise room, across the other hall and into the makeshift nursery, where a small night-light burned. Mona was sitting up in her crib, her mouth open and her face streaming with tears as she sobbed her dissatisfaction. As Jolie approached, speaking softly, the little one flopped onto her back, a sure sign that she needed a dry diaper.

Jolie made quick work of the diaper, and Mona quieted as she did so, but when Jolie turned her onto her side and attempted to get her back to sleep by gently patting her back as Dessie had often instructed, Mona sat up and began to cry again. Jolie lifted the child into her arms, and Mona instantly hushed and laid her head on Jolie's shoulder. Jolie stood for several moments, humming softly and swaying side to side in an effort to coax Mona back to sleep.

"I have a rocking chair in my room." Chan's voice came from the shadows beyond the doorway. "I thought about bringing it in here, but it's so wide that the door casings have to come off to move it from room to room."

The quiet, gentle tones washed over Jolie like a soothing breeze. She turned a smile over one shoulder and replied softly, "Let's give this a few minutes." But it soon became obvious that *this* was not working, even though Mona rubbed her eyes and whimpered tiredly against Jolie's shoulder. It was an exhausting exercise, as well. "Perhaps we'd better try that rocker, after all."

He stepped forward, wearing baggy gym shorts and a shapeless T-shirt, and lifted Mona's considerable weight from Jolie's arms, carrying her back to his room while Jolie followed silently. A light shone dimly beside his bed across the large room, and an opened hardback book lay face down on the rumpled chocolate-brown sheets. Channing carried Mona across the sitting area to the wide, low-backed, well-padded rocking chair upholstered in faux zebra skin. He waited until Jolie sat, then placed Mona on her lap. Mona gazed around her sleepily, then lay back in Jolie's arms, turned her face against Jolie's chest and relaxed. Jolie concentrated on rocking the baby, occasionally humming as she did so. Before long, Mona was a dead weight in her arms, her deep, even breathing a testament to the depth of her slumber.

Carefully, Jolie slid to the edge of the seat of the chair and rocked forward. Channing instantly stepped up to help her to her feet, then silently steered her toward the door. Jolie smiled her thanks and padded out into the hall. He didn't follow, and she carried Mona back to her crib alone, carefully put her down and waited several minutes to be certain that the baby had finally settled into sleep. Confident the child would sleep for some time now, Jolie returned the way she had come. Just as she stepped into the darkened hallway outside her bedroom, Channing again spoke from the heavy shadows.

"That was quite a sight." He stepped forward, close enough that she could make out the baggy white T-shirt that he wore. She hugged herself, not because she was chilled but because the sound of his voice had done strange things to her skin. It was as if he literally touched her in many places at once. She had to concentrate to make a reply.

"Hm? What was?"

"You rocking the baby."

She said nothing to that, uncertain what she ought to say, what he expected, and after a moment he went on in the same velvety voice.

"Phil never had that. Oh, Donnelly might have rocked her, probably did, but her mother never did. No woman ever did." He sighed, obviously remembering. "She thought she was too big for it when she came to me. Mona's the only child who's ever been rocked in that chair. I quite enjoyed watching you do it."

Jolie couldn't just stand there, allowing his voice to infiltrate her body. She had to say something. "L-let's hope she's finally down for the night."

"I'd love to see you rocking our child like that," he said, just as if she hadn't spoken at all. "I think you'd be a wonderful mother."

The idea swam around her head, leaving a comet tail of sparkling dreams and desires that she had barely acknowledged until he'd spoken. *Our child.* She gasped, aware suddenly of all that she was losing, all the possibilities and probabilities that ceased to exist when she finally, somehow, walked away from him.

He stepped close and wrapped his arms around her, drawing her against him. "Forget the damned contract," he said roughly. "Just marry me. If you really don't want another child, I can live with that. I have Phil, after all. Just don't throw away everything that we could have together."

Forget the contract? A sudden, inexplicable joy suffused her. He was willing to forget the contract? But then why marry unless… No, he didn't love her, and without that she had even less reason to marry him than before. It would be sheer insanity to marry him now, but the very reason for that was the same one that had her sliding her arms about his waist, holding on to him when she should be pushing him away.

He lifted his hands to frame her face, his fingers sliding into her hair. *One night,* she told herself. *One night.* She could have that much, couldn't she? Why not? Other women did it all the time.

But even as he lowered his mouth to hers, she knew that she couldn't do it. She could never allow herself such folly. One night would only leave her bereft, always wanting more, regretting what could never be and should not have been. The kiss, however, she could not refuse, especially as it carried a kind of sweetness she'd never before felt or tasted.

His long arms held her tightly as his mouth mated with hers, his tongue finding spots of intense sensitivity to probe and stroke. She clutched her fists in the back of his shirt and gave as good as she got, losing herself for this one exquisite moment. When his mouth left hers and traveled a burning trail across her jaw to her ear and then down the sensitive column of her neck, she let her head fall back, moaning her enjoyment as he nipped and kissed and laved her skin. Nudging aside the neck of her pajama top with his nose, he carefully sank his teeth into the top of her shoulder, breathing moist fire against her skin. Her knees buckled, hot waves of sensation washing over her, so that she leaned into him more solidly, her breasts spreading against his chest.

Dipping, he caught her up, one arm beneath her knees and the other about her shoulders. She looped her arms about his neck reflexively and barely noticed that he was moving until she felt him bend toward the bed. He placed her on her back and came down on top of her, his mouth finding hers unerringly. He was heavier than she'd expected, somehow more solid, more *male,* but far from being unpleasant, his weight atop her felt right, exciting, especially when he pressed himself between her legs, allowing her to feel the long, steely ridge of his desire. They ought not to be here like this, she knew. Soon she would send him away, but not yet. Oh, not yet.

He braced his upper body on his elbows, and framed her face with his hands. She couldn't see his expression as well as she might have wished, but she could feel, and what she felt threatened to set the bed aflame. He eased himself upward and brought his mouth down over hers once more, fitting them together with exquisite care. For a long, lovely moment, he held himself still, but then his hips flexed, and he drove his tongue into her mouth, making the flames explode around them. In short order she found herself being devoured and burned alive in the same instant, and all she wanted was more, more, more of the same.

Levering his weight to one side, he covered her breast with his hand. She could not resist the urge to arch her back, and suddenly she was panting between frantic kisses. He ground against her, moaning deep in his chest. Then suddenly his hand was shoving her top up and his mouth was on her breast. She had never felt anything like it. The wonder of sensation in parts of her body as yet untouched literally knocked her back into the mattress, and then he slid his hand between her legs, demonstrating that he knew exactly what he was doing to her, and the shock of his fingers against her most intimate flesh had her scurrying for purchase on the bed, finally finding it, and shoving herself upward. She yanked her top down as he stiffly rolled and lifted himself to sit next to her.

"Jolie—" he began, but she cut him off, knowing that if he pressed the matter she would be unable to refuse him.

"You should go," she croaked, swinging her legs off the side of the bed.

"Please listen to me a moment," he begged. "I've been so foolish. I know now that—"

She imagined a dozen endings to that sentence. *I made a mistake. It would never work between us. I need more than a contracted marriage can deliver. We would do better as lovers and friends than spouses.* She could not bear to hear any of them, not just then.

"Please go," she said firmly.

He came off the bed. "Damn it, Jolie!"

"Just go!" she shouted, desperate to have him gone now,

before she broke down in a blubbering heap and poured out her heart, leaving herself with nothing, not even her pride.

Angrily, he drove a hand through his hair, then strode from the room, swinging through the open doorway with one hand clamped around the frame on one side. Jolie stood as she was, holding herself together with her arms wrapped tightly about her middle, until she heard his bedroom door slam. Only then did she slowly lower herself to sit on the edge of the bed and allow the tears to flow.

She managed to pretend for all of Saturday and most of Sunday that nothing had happened between them in the wee hours after Friday night. If she occasionally caught Channing staring at her with sad eyes, Jolie chose to ignore it, afraid of what it might mean, and she was careful to avoid being alone with him for even a moment. On Saturday she moved into the room next to Mona's and stayed there, even though the baby seemed to have settled in.

Sadie came, and Jolie had a nice chat with her mother, who sang Phil's praises loudly. Obviously Phil's intelligence and maturity made her the perfect friend for Sadie, who, like Phil, had her own problems fitting in. It seemed that the two of them were writing a play, though the subject matter was a closely held secret for the time being. Jolie reveled from a distance in the giggling byplay between the two, sorrowfully aware that this might well be her last opportunity to witness it.

She packed her bag on Sunday morning and left it beside the bedroom door, marking the hours until Dessie and Ben returned late in the day. Phil and Channing made a huge breakfast of something they called Dutch Babies, a cross between a pancake and a soufflé, filled with spiced apples and served with blueberry syrup. Jolie did her best but could only manage a few bites before the urge to escape Channing's solemn gaze became too much to bear.

Dessie and Ben didn't help her mood any. They seemed so happy, so very much in love when they arrived more than an hour late, thanks to a flight delay. Jolie found herself resenting the way they snuggled together on the couch and seemed to finish each other's sentences as they talked about their trip. They laughed about the way the elderly Justice of the Peace had botched their vows. They spoke of standing in the cool spray of the falls at night and counting the stars overhead, of sleeping so very, very well in a too-small bed and of missing Mona, whom they cuddled and kissed and tickled. Jolie felt small and guilty for the animosity, the sheer envy, that ate at her. She hoped that she managed not to show her feelings and was relieved to find that she sincerely did wish them well.

The very instant that the door closed behind them, Jolie headed upstairs to collect her single bag and make her own escape. Unfortunately, she returned to the stairwell to find Channing blocking her way, one shoulder leaning against the rough stone wall.

"You're not going anywhere until we talk," he said implacably.

Desperation and panic seized her, but she did her best to cover. "We can talk later," she said. *Much, much later.* "I have a lot to do before—"

"Now," he insisted. "We're going to talk now."

Anger flared, purely defensive, but she welcomed it, nonetheless. "How dare you try to tell me what to do?"

"Running away," he snapped, "isn't going to do any good."

"I'm not!"

"The hell you're not!"

"Don't you shout at me!"

"I'm not the only one shouting!"

She ground her teeth, knowing he was right but feeling perfectly justified. "Get out of my way," she demanded, shoving past him. He caught her by the arm, and the handle of her small, soft-sided bag popped out of her hand. The bag tumbled down the stairs. Jolie watched it, mouth gaping open, until it rounded the curve and fell out of sight. Truly enraged now, she stamped her foot. "Now look what you've done!"

His tone was unapologetic. "I was just trying to make you see reason."

Suddenly all she could see was red. "You…you… lunatic! You wouldn't know reason if it bit you on the butt! This whole stupid business was your doing from start to finish. You came up with this contract nonsense."

"Yes, and you agreed!" he shot back. "Seems to me that makes us a pair of lunatics, a matched set. And I don't have to let you out of our current contract, by the way. Were I of a mind to, I could—"

"Don't you threaten me, Channing Hawkins!"

"I'm not! I'm trying to tell you that I love you!"

Jolie's heart made a pronounced *thump* in her chest and then just seemed to stop. For a moment she was too stunned to do anything but gape. Gradually, she realized that he was staring down at her expectantly. She watched him swallow and lick his lips in a gesture so nervous that she cocked her head, momentarily puzzled. Then suddenly she knew. The poor man had been fighting the same demons and doubts that she had! She didn't let him fight them any longer. "Oh, Channing, I love you, too." He closed his eyes and sagged in relief.

"Woo-hoo!" Obviously eavesdropping, Phil came flying

up the stairs. "It's about time! I don't know who's more stubborn, Jolie or you, Dad!"

Jolie caught her breath and shot a glance at Channing. For a moment he just stared at Phil, but then he switched his gaze to Jolie, and a smile tugged at one corner of his mouth. He cleared his throat. "It's 'Dad' now, is it?"

Jolie pressed her back to the wall so she could see them both and carefully divided her attention. Phil looked down at her toes, hunched a shoulder and mumbled, "Having a dad's not such a bad thing." She shot a glance at Jolie and added, "Provided you've got a mom to go with him."

Jolie caught her breath. "Oh, Phil," she whispered, "I don't know if—"

"I do," Channing interrupted, coming down the stairs toward her. He stopped on the step next to Jolie and cupped her face in his big hands. "Phil's right," he said. "We need a mom around here. But *I* need more than that. I desperately need a wife. As long as it's you."

Her vision clouded with tears. "Channing!"

"Will you marry me, Jolie?"

"You know I will!" She threw her arms at him and somehow managed to hook one about his neck, and then she was being pulled up and into a fierce embrace. He bent his head and brought his mouth to hers. She went up on tiptoe to meet him, pouring her heart into that kiss.

"I guess we can forget that stupid contract," Phil said smugly.

Channing lifted his head and looked at Jolie. They both started to laugh. "What contract?" he quipped, and kissed her again. Only when they teetered on the step did he break away to swing her up into his arms. Turning, he vaulted up the stairs to the landing, where he swung her around, spinning on his heels. Then suddenly he froze. Jolie looked down to find Phil smiling up at them, tears running down her face. Jolie nudged Channing, and he dropped one arm, letting her feet slide to the floor.

"Phil," she said, holding out her arms. The girl ran up the stairs and into her embrace, sobs breaking out as she buried her face against Jolie's chest.

"What's wrong, honey?" Channing asked gently, his hand settling in the space between her shoulder blades.

She sniffed and shook her head. "It's silly."

"More silly than trying to make love and marriage into a business deal?" he asked wryly.

She lifted her head. "Not *that* silly," she admitted.

Jolie bit back a chuckle and cupped the girl's chin with one hand. "Why don't you tell us what it is?"

Phil sighed. "It's just, suddenly everything's so...*n-n-normal!*" she wailed.

Jolie glanced at Chan, whose eyes were glittering suspiciously. "Normal isn't so bad, is it?" she asked Phil softly.

Phil stepped back and threw her arms wide. "Normal is wonderful!" she exclaimed. Then, as Channing's hands fell upon Jolie's shoulders possessively, Phil made a face, dashed away the tears with one hand and exclaimed, "Even if I do have to watch kissy-face stuff from now on."

"So don't watch," Channing said meaningfully, tugging Jolie toward his bedroom.

Phil stuck out her tongue as he swept Jolie along before him, but she was laughing when he closed the door. They heard her singing an age-old childhood ditty.

"Mom and Dad sitting in a tree, k-i-s-s-i-n-g!"

Neither made comment. They were much too busy discovering that Phil was right. Normal was delightful. And love did what no contract ever could. It laid fears to rest, grew courage in hearts already full and gave permission to risk all even as it loosed the reins on desire and need.

Jolie was still frightened. Marriage still seemed a chancy,

foolish business. But she knew now that for a man and woman in love, it was the only real option, perhaps the only actual hope, the only way to real family, to forever. And in a way, love itself was a contract, a pledge, a choice to try and keep on trying. No wonder her parents had spent their lives searching for such a love as this. No wonder Dessie and Ben had found the courage to try again.

Mom and Dad sitting in a tree, k-i-s-s-i-n-g.

No doubt Phil would teach that tune to her brothers and sisters. Jolie could hardly wait. Well, maybe a little while.

* * * * *

Don't miss the next novel
from beloved author Arlene James:
THE DETECTIVE'S DILEMMA,
part of MAITLAND MATERNITY,
on sale January 2001.

Beloved author

JOAN ELLIOTT PICKART

reprises her successful miniseries

THE BABY BET

with the following delightful stories:

On sale June 2000

TO A MACALLISTER BORN

Silhouette Special Edition® #1329

The Bachelor Bet's Jennifer Mackane proves more than a match for marriage-wary Jack MacAllister.

On Sale July 2000

THE BABY BET: HIS SECRET SON

Silhouette Books®

A secret son stirs up trouble for patriarch Robert MacAllister and the clan.

On sale October 2000

BABY: MACALLISTER-MADE

Silhouette Desire® #1326

A night of passion has bachelor Richard MacAllister awaiting the next bouncing MacAllister bundle!

And coming to Special Edition® in 2001:

HER LITTLE SECRET.

Available at your favorite retail outlet.

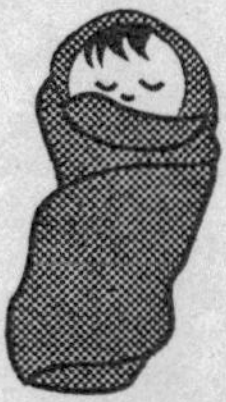

Silhouette®

Where love comes alive™

Visit Silhouette at www.eHarlequin.com

PSBET

A brooding monarch.
A playboy prince.
A rebellious princess.

Meet the de Marigny ruling family in
Valerie Parv's

THE CARRAMER CROWN

One by one, royal siblings discover passion
more powerful than any monarchy.

On sale July 2000
THE MONARCH'S SON
Silhouette Romance® #1459

On sale August 2000
THE PRINCE'S BRIDE-TO-BE
Silhouette Romance® #1465

On sale September 2000
THE PRINCESS'S PROPOSAL
Silhouette Romance® #1471

Available at your favorite retail outlet.

Silhouette®
Where love comes alive™

Visit Silhouette at www.eHarlequin.com SRTCC

Don't miss an exciting opportunity to save on the purchase of Harlequin and Silhouette books!

Buy any two Harlequin or Silhouette books and save **$10.00 off** future Harlequin and Silhouette purchases

OR

buy any three Harlequin or Silhouette books and save **$20.00 off** future Harlequin and Silhouette purchases.

Watch for details coming in October 2000!

PHQ400

HARLEQUIN®
Makes any time special™

Silhouette®
Where love comes alive™

Silhouette

where love comes alive—online...

your romantic
life

➢ Talk to Dr. Romance, find a romantic recipe, or send a virtual hint to the love of your life. You'll find great articles and advice on romantic issues that are close to your heart.

your romantic
books

➢ Visit our *Author's Alcove* and try your hand in the Writing Round Robin—contribute a chapter to an online book in the making.

➢ Enter the *Reading Room* for an interactive novel—help determine the fate of a story being created now by one of your favorite authors.

➢ Drop into *Shop eHarlequin* to buy the latest releases—read an excerpt, write a review and find this month's Silhouette top sellers.

your romantic
escapes

➢ Escape into romantic movies at *Reel Love,* learn what the stars have in store for you with *Lovescopes,* treat yourself to our *Indulgences Guides* and get away to the latest romantic hot spots in *Romantic Travel.*

All this and more available at
www.eHarlequin.com
on Women.com Networks

SECHAN1R

Celebrate 20 YEARS

Intimate Moments is celebrating Silhouette's 20th Anniversary with groundbreaking new promotions and star authors:

Look for these original novels from
New York Times bestselling authors:

In August 2000:
A Game of Chance by **Linda Howard**, #1021

In September 2000:
Night Shield by **Nora Roberts**,
part of NIGHT TALES

Don't miss
A YEAR OF LOVING DANGEROUSLY,
a twelve-book continuity series featuring SPEAR—a covert intelligence agency. For its equally enigmatic operatives, love was never part of the mission profile.... **Sharon Sala** launches the promotion in July 2000 with *Mission: Irresistible*, #1016.

In September 2000, look for the return of **36 HOURS**, with original stories from **Susan Mallery**, **Margaret Watson**, **Doreen Roberts** and **Marilyn Pappano**.

And look for:
Who Do You Love?
October 2000, #1033
You won't want to miss this two-in-one collection featuring **Maggie Shayne** and **Marilyn Pappano**!

Available at your favorite retail outlet.

Silhouette®
Where love comes alive™

Celebrate 20 YEARS

Visit Silhouette at www.eHarlequin.com

PS20SIM

Silhouette invites you to come back to Whitehorn, Montana...

MONTANA MAVERICKS

WED IN WHITEHORN—
12 BRAND-NEW stories that capture living and loving beneath the Big Sky where legends live on and love lasts forever!

MM

June 2000—
Lisa Jackson *Lone Stallion's Lady* (#1)

July 2000—
Laurie Paige *Cheyenne Bride* (#2)

August 2000—
Jennifer Greene *You Belong to Me* (#3)

September 2000—
Victoria Pade *The Marriage Bargain* (#4)

And the adventure continues...

Available at your favorite retail outlet.

Silhouette®
Where love comes alive™

Visit Silhouette at www.eHarlequin.com PSMMGEN1

Silhouette ROMANCE™

COMING NEXT MONTH

#1468 HIS EXPECTANT NEIGHBOR—Susan Meier
Storkville, USA
The *last* thing loner Ben Crowe wanted was a beautiful single woman renting the cottage on his ranch—and a pregnant one at that! Yet when Gwen Parker gave him her sweet smile, how could he refuse? And how could he guard his hardened heart?

#1469 MARRYING MADDY—Kasey Michaels
The Chandlers Request...
It was one week before Maddy Chandler's wedding to a safe, sensible man, and she should have been ecstatic. But then her former love Joe O'Malley suddenly moved in right next door, with plans to show lovely Maddy *he* was the groom for her!

#1470 DADDY IN DRESS BLUES—Cathie Linz
When Curt Blackwell went to check out his daughter's new preschool, he was surprised to find that her enticing teacher, Jessica Moore, was "Jessie the Brain" from their high school days! Suddenly Curt was looking forward to staying after school....

#1471 THE PRINCESS'S PROPOSAL—Valerie Parv
The Carramer Crown
Brains, beauty…a prize stallion—Princess Adrienne de Marigny had Hugh Jordan's every desire. And he had a little something *she* wanted. The princess's proposal involved a competition, winner take all. But the plan backfired, leading to a different proposal....

#1472 A GLEAM IN HIS EYE—Terry Essig
Johanna Durbin was on her own after helping raise her siblings—and intended to enjoy single life. That is, until she met sexy guardian Hunter Pace, who needed daddy lessons—fast! But was Hunter looking for a temporary stint…or a family forever?

#1473 THE LIBRARIAN'S SECRET WISH—Carol Grace
Tough, brooding, calloused—and devilishly handsome—investigator Nate Callahan was the kind of guy librarian Claire Cooper had learned to stay away from. Still, how could she turn her back on a missing little boy? Or on a chance to feel the love she'd always dreamed of…?